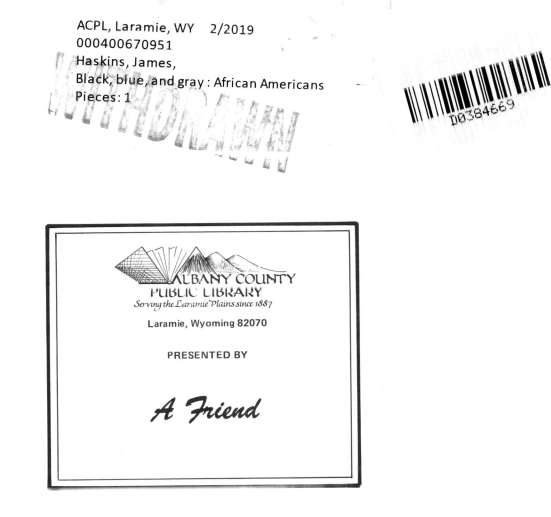

Black, Blue & Gray

African Americans in the Civil War

Black, Blue & Gray

African Americans in the Civil War

Jim Haskins

Simon & Schuster Books for Young Readers

Acknowledgments

I am grateful to Kathy Benson, Ann Kalkhoff, and Bill Rice for their help.

SIMON & SCHUSTER BOOKS FOR YOUNG READERS
An imprint of Simon & Schuster Children's Publishing Division
1230 Avenue of the Americas, New York, New York 10020
Text copyright © 1998 by James Haskins

Book design by Symon Chow
The text for this book is set in 12-point Golden Cockerel.
Printed and bound in the United States of America
First Edition
10 9 8 7 6 5 4 3 2 1
Library of Congress Cataloging-in-Publication Data
Haskins, James, 1941-
Black, blue, and gray : African Americans in the Civil War / Jim Haskins.
p.   cm.
Includes bibliographical references (p. 148) and index.
Summary: An historical account of the role of African-American soldiers in the Civil War.
ISBN 0-689-80655-8
1. United States—History—Civil War, 1861-1865—Participation, Afro-American—Juvenile literature. 2. United States—History—Civil War, 1861-1865—Afro-Americans—Juvenile literature. 3. Afro-Americans—History—To 1863—Juvenile literature. 4. Afro-Americans—History—1863-1877—Juvenile literature. [1. United States—History—Civil War, 1861-1865—Participation, Afro-American. 2. United States—History, Civil War, 1861-1865—Afro-Americans. 3. Afro-Americans—History—To 1863. 4. Afro-Americans—History-1863-1877. 5. Afro-American soldiers—History. 6. Soldiers.] I. Title.
E540.N3H37 1998
973.7'415—dc21
97-25414

Contents

Introduction

A "White Man's War"?

In 1775 the first shots were fired in the war between the thirteen American colonies and Great Britain that ended in a victory for the colonists and the founding of a new nation, the United States of America. Only eighty-five years later, in 1861, the first shots were fired in a different war—a war between the states that became known as the Civil War. It was a war fought between the Confederate States of America—seven southern states that had seceded from the United States of America—and the states that remained in the Union, each side representing a distinct economy, labor system, and philosophy of government. The southern states that formed the Confederacy had agricultural economies that depended on a slave workforce and believed that any rights not granted to the federal government by the United States Constitution belonged to the states. The northern states were undergoing rapid industrialization, which depended on wage labor, and while northerners disagreed among themselves about slavery, most believed that it represented a direct challenge to their own rights and freedoms. Most also believed that a strong federal government, with the ability to legislate behavior in areas not specifically set forth in the Constitution, was key to the growth and strength of the American republic. It was inevitable that these two very distinct societies would clash. For the Confederates, nicknamed Rebels, the Civil War was a new war of independence. For the Unionists, nicknamed Yankees, it was a war to preserve the Union that had been so dearly won in the American Revolution.

In the eyes of the four and a half million African Americans, enslaved and free, it was a war about slavery; and they wanted to be part of the fight. But many northern whites did not want blacks to serve in the northern military. They called it a "white man's war" and said that slavery was not the main point of the conflict. At first, northern generals actually sent escaped slaves back to their southern masters. Eventually, the Union did accept blacks into its army and navy.

A total of 178,895 black men served in 120 infantry regiments, twelve heavy artillery regiments, ten light artillery batteries, and seven cavalry regiments. Black soldiers constituted twelve percent of the North's fighting forces, and they suffered a disproportionate number of casualties.

The efforts of the black soldiers tipped the balance in favor of the Union side. The Civil War ended with a Union victory over the Confederacy in 1865 and for a few years afterward the contributions of blacks in the Civil War were common knowledge. But by 1928 some white American historians had so thoroughly rewritten history that a man named W. E. Woodward stated in a biography of Ulysses S. Grant, the Union general who later became president, "the American negroes are the only people in the history of the world, so far as I know, that ever became free without any effort of their own. . . . [The Civil War] was not their business. They had not started the war nor ended it. They twanged banjos around the railroad stations, sang melodious spirituals, and believed that some Yankees would soon come along and give each of them forty acres of land and a mule." [1]

If those were the facts so far as Woodward knew, then he did not know much. African Americans had not been able to prevent slavery. But when war over slavery did come, they played a major role. On the Civil War battlefields, blacks fought not only on the side of the blue, the official color of most Union uniforms, but also on the side of the gray, the official color of the Confederate troops. In the end, it was a black man's war as much as it was "a white man's war."

One

"But This Question Is Still to Be Settled—This Negro Question, I Mean . . ."

Slavery had been a source of controversy since colonial times. Although slaves were employed in both northern and southern colonies, it was the southern colonies that developed strong, agriculture-based economies that required thousands of slaves to maintain the rice, cotton, and, later, sugarcane plantations. Faced with a majority slave population and with periodic slave revolts, such as the Stono, South Carolina, Rebellion in 1739, most southern whites persuaded themselves that slaves were subhuman and not capable of being educated, much less free. The comparatively small population of free blacks in the South sometimes faced greater hardships than their slave counterparts.

While many northerners shared the attitude that blacks were subhuman, slaves in the North tended to be few by comparison to the South and they were more likely to be educated and learn skilled trades and to have greater opportunities to earn money to purchase their freedom. By the time of the Revolutionary War in 1775, freed slaves and freeborn African Americans in the North had organized their own churches and self-help societies. And when the thirteen colonies began to call for freedom from Great Britain, many northern blacks called for their own freedom. But the 1776 Declaration of Independence contained not one word about slaves or slavery.

Blacks, slave and free, fought and died in the American Revolution. In the years following the war, before the Constitution was written and ratified by the former colonies, blacks fervently hoped that the atmosphere of independence would cause whites to look more kindly on them. At the convention to draw up a Constitution for the new nation, representatives from the thirteen new states engaged in heated debate over slavery. At that time slavery was legal in all thirteen colonies, but many northern delegates to the Constitutional Convention believed that slavery contradicted the ideas stated in the Declaration of Independence, namely "all men are created equal." The southern delegates, intent on preserving slavery, the backbone of the southern economy, disagreed that slaves were men. Instead, they believed slaves were chattel, or property. The writers of the Constitution could not agree on the issue. In order to reach a consensus on uniting the states under one federal government, they chose to ignore the paradox of slavery in a free nation. The words *slave* and *slavery* are nowhere to be found in either the Constitution or the Bill of Rights (the first ten amendments to that document), only references to "persons owing service or labor."

To hold the nation, then called the Union, together, northern and southern states struggled to create some balance of power. Because the northern states had larger populations, they would have had more congressmen, according to the system of proportional representation in the House of Representatives. To ensure an equal voice in Congress, the southern states insisted that, for purposes of representation in the government, a slave be counted as three-fifths of a man. Not only did this so-called "Three-fifths Compromise" give the southern states equivalent representation; it also gave them the votes to prevent any attempt by the North to outlaw slavery. For the next three-quarters of a century, that uneasy balance was maintained at all costs as slavery continued to be a point of conflict between northern and southern states. Every time a new state was admitted to the Union, the risk of tipping that balance arose anew.

While the members of Congress, in Washington, D.C., worked to keep the balance, abolitionists made every attempt to upset it. The organized movement of people who believed that slavery should be outlawed, or abolished, grew as the nineteenth century wore on. Whites and blacks wrote and spoke against slavery, formed societies to spread their philosophy, and started political parties whose main platform was the abolition of slavery. By the 1820s, slavery had been abolished in most of the northern states. In the South, abolitionism was against the law.

As time went on, more and more southern slaves took their future in their own hands and escaped slavery, running away from their

Frederick Douglass lived to see the end of slavery and the brief moment during Reconstruction when southern blacks were allowed to vote and even hold office. He died in 1895, just before the United States Supreme Court decision in Plessy v. Ferguson upheld separate-but-equal accommodations, and thus was spared the painful knowledge that his people would be treated, by law, as second-class citizens. (Library of Congress)

southern masters and heading north. Frederick Douglass was among them. Born Frederick Bailey, a slave, in 1817 in Maryland, he received his first lessons in reading and writing from his master's wife. After his master put a stop to that, saying that education would make the boy unfit to be a slave, Frederick continued his education in secret. At the age of twenty-one, presenting himself as a freeborn sailor, he escaped to New York City. From there he went to New Bedford, Massachusetts, where he changed his last name to Douglass.

In New Bedford, Douglass worked as a laborer on the docks until, three years later, in 1841, he was invited to speak to an antislavery convention on Nantucket Island, Massachusetts, about his feelings and experiences in slavery. A tall, handsome man with a massive head made even larger by a huge mane of black hair, Douglass's presence was commanding. He spoke with great eloquence, and his story was so poignant that he soon had a new career as an abolitionist spokesman. In the course of his career as an abolitionist, he published a series of newspapers in which he gave his views on issues affecting African Americans.

Douglass was active in the Underground Railroad, a network of abolitionists, Quakers, and others established by the 1830s to help fugitive slaves escape bondage. The "tracks" of this railroad usually began in

Harriet Tubman, the most famous conductor on the Underground Railroud, was credited with bringing more than three hundred people out of southern slavery. After the Civil War broke out, and activity on the Underground Railroad ceased, Tubman acted as a scout for Union troops and helped the "contrabands" in slave refugee camps behind Union lines. (Schomburg Center for Research in Black Culture, New York Public Library)

the border slaveholding states of Delaware, Maryland, Kentucky, Missouri, and the counties of Virginia that would become West Virginia. "Railroad stations" were the homes of other slaves or freedmen, or of sympathetic whites. The "stationmasters" fed the fugitives and offered them a safe place to sleep, then directed them to the next station. In many instances, the final stop was Canada, where slavery was illegal.

Underground Railroad activity infuriated slave owners. Every time a slave escaped, a valuable investment was lost, not to mention the labor that the slave had provided. Slave owners placed advertisements in newspapers, describing their runaways and offering rewards of anywhere from four dollars for a child to one hundred dollars for the capture of an adult male. Professional slave hunters were in the business of capturing the runaway slaves and collecting those rewards.

Sometimes slave hunters were not too particular about whom they caught. There were cases in which free blacks in the North were captured by slave hunters and sold into slavery. In many northern communities, people did all they could to prevent slave hunters from doing their business.

By the 1850s, confrontations between slave hunters and people trying to protect fugitive slaves became more frequent—and more violent. Southern states succeeded in pushing through federal fugitive slave laws providing for punishment of anyone who helped a slave to escape. But northern states frequently countered the federal fugitive laws with their own laws guaranteeing the rights of individuals.

With the *Dred Scott* case, the confrontation over slavery and states' rights reached the United States Supreme Court.

Dred Scott, born Sam Blow, was a slave belonging to Peter Blow, a Virginia planter. Following the War of 1812, fought by the United States and Great Britain over control of trade in the Atlantic and British presence in Canada, the state of Virginia suffered a severe economic depression. Like many other Virginia planters, Peter Blow moved his family and slaves south to Alabama. By 1820, however, Peter Blow had concluded that he could barely eke out a living in Alabama, so he and his family and slaves moved once again, this time to St. Louis, Missouri. Some ten years later, Peter Blow died, leaving many debts. To help pay off the debts, the Blow slave Sam was sold at public auction. He was purchased by Dr. John Emerson, a graduate of the University of Pennsylvania Medical School. Dr. Emerson received an army commission soon afterward and, taking his family and slaves with him, reported for duty as post surgeon at Fort Armstrong, Illinois, around 1833.

Three years later, the doctor was posted to Wisconsin Territory and again took his family and slaves with him.

Dr. Emerson died suddenly, and his wife returned to St. Louis with the rest of the family and their slaves. Three years after their return, the slave Sam, who now insisted on being called Dred Scott, demanded that Dr. Emerson's widow sell him his freedom. When she refused, he sued her. His lawyers argued that his onetime residence in the free state of Illinois and in the Territory of Wisconsin, where slavery was also not allowed, had made him a free man.

The case, called *Scott* v. [against] *Sandiford*, went all the way to the United States Supreme Court, whose responsibility was deciding the law of the land based on the United States Constitution. In 1857, the Court ruled that Scott was not a citizen and thus had no right to bring suit in the courts.

Pro-slavery forces applauded the Court's decision. Abolitionists despaired of it. In effect, the decision meant that Congress could not outlaw slavery anywhere.

But Frederick Douglass saw it as a means of further galvanizing the antislavery movement. He wrote, "We the abolitionists and colored people, should meet this decision, monstrous as it appears, in a cheerful spirit. This very attempt to blot out forever the hopes of an enslaved people may be one necessary link in the chain of events preparatory to the complete overthrow of the whole slave system." [1]

In 1859, two years after the Supreme Court's decision in *Scott* v. *Sandiford*, a white abolitionist named John Brown attempted to overthrow the slave system. Brown led a raid on the federal arsenal at Harpers Ferry, Virginia, planning to seize the arms stored there, liberate the slaves in the surrounding area, and then establish a base in Virginia's Allegheny Mountains from which to defend the fugitive slaves and lead additional raids against slavery. Brown even drafted a constitution for his community, which called for all property to be held in common. Brown's raid was put down, and Brown himself was hanged. But before he was put to death, he spoke some very prophetic words, warning the leaders of the South: "You may dispose of me very easily, I am nearly disposed of now. But this question is still to be settled   this Negro question, I mean; the end of that is not yet. You had better—all you people at the South—prepare yourselves for a settlement of this question." [2]

On the political front, the Supreme Court decision in the 1857 *Dred Scott* case prompted more northerners to join the new Republican Party, which was formed primarily to fight the expansion of slavery into

President Abraham Lincoln; photograph by Mathew Brady. (Library of Congress)

the Western territories and which three years later selected Abraham Lincoln of Illinois as its presidential candidate.

Lincoln had previously served one term in Congress (1847–49) and had not been well-known on the national scene until 1858, when he ran against Democrat Stephen A. Douglas for the Illinois senate. By this time, Lincoln had been caught up in the debate over slavery and was convinced that the issue threatened to destroy the union of states. He had joined the Republican Party in 1856. In accepting the Republican Party's nomination for the senate seat two years later, he declared, "A house divided against itself cannot stand."

During the senatorial campaign, Lincoln had challenged Douglas to a series of debates. During those seven debates, which focused solely on slavery, he proved so eloquent in his arguments against enslavement that, although he lost the election, he won many admirers in the national Republican Party. By the time of the 1860 election, slavery was *the* national issue.

Lincoln was not an abolitionist. Although he regarded slavery as unfair and unjust, he wanted nothing more than to exclude it from the territories. His moderate stand appealed to many who could not agree with extreme positions on either side of the slavery issue. Lincoln was elected president in November 1860, even though he won only a minority of the popular vote.

At the time of Abraham Lincoln's election, according to the 1860 census, the population of the United States was 31,364,367. Whites were in the vast majority, totaling nearly 27 million. There were nearly 4 million slaves, and just under half a million free blacks. The issue of slavery had become so heated that no compromise seemed possible. In fact, in the eyes of southerners, Lincoln's election was a signal that slavery's days were numbered.

Rather than see slavery ended, several southern states preferred to secede, or separate, from the United States and form their own nation. By December 1860, South Carolina had taken the step of seceding, and it was soon followed by six other southern states: Florida, Alabama, Georgia, Louisiana, Mississippi, and Texas. By the time Lincoln was inaugurated the sixteenth president of the United States, on March 4, 1861, the Union was seven states smaller than it had been at his election.

The seven states formed a new nation, the Confederate States of America. On February 4, 1861, delegates from the states met in Montgomery, Alabama, and elected a president, Jefferson Davis, of

Mississippi, and a vice president, Alexander Stephens, of Georgia. On March 11, one week after President Abraham Lincoln was inaugurated, the Confederate States adopted a constitution containing states' rights provisions and recognizing and protecting slavery.

As part of the newly independent nation, South Carolina wished to control everything within its borders. That included the new federal Fort Sumter, still under construction as part of the defense facilities of the United States on a man-made granite island in Charleston harbor. Since its secession from the Union in late 1860, South Carolina had been pressing the federal government to give up the fort. The outgoing U.S. president, James A. Buchanan, had done nothing. He was afraid to give up the fort because it would anger northerners; at the same time, he was afraid that sending additional federal troops to protect the fort would anger southerners.

By the time Lincoln took office, it was quite evident to nearly everyone that the Union and the Confederacy would go to war. The logical first battleground was Charleston harbor, where the disputed Fort Sumter was still manned by a small garrison of federal troops. By this time, the troops at Fort Sumter had almost run out of supplies and had to be reprovisioned. Because the fort was federal property, Lincoln regarded it as still part of the Union, and he wanted to send additional federal troops, guns, and ammunition to strengthen the garrison. But he feared that doing so would be taken as an act of war against the Confederacy and might cause some or all of the eight slaveholding border states also to secede from the Union and join the Confederacy. Instead, he notified the governor of South Carolina that the federal government was sending a relief fleet to the fort, carrying provisions only, and if Confederate forces attacked the fleet, the Confederacy would be responsible for the first hostile action between the Union and the Confederacy.

In response, Confederate president Jefferson Davis ordered General Pierre T. Beauregard to take the fort before the provision fleet arrived.

On April 12, 1861, Confederate forces fired on Fort Sumter. President Lincoln called for troops to defend the Union, and four border states—Arkansas, North Carolina, Tennessee, and Virginia—joined the Confederacy. The Civil War was on.

It was a war waged by the North to preserve the Union and by the South to defend its independence. In the minds of most Americans, it was not a war over slavery. But in the opinion of Frederick Douglass and many other abolitionists, slavery was the main issue. As Douglass wrote in *Douglass' Monthly* in 1861: "Any attempt now to separate the freedom of the slave from the victory of the Government, . . . any attempt to secure peace to the whites while leaving the blacks in chains . . . will be labor lost. The American people and the Government at Washington may refuse to recognize it for a time; but the 'inexorable logic of events' will force it upon them in the end; that the war now being waged in this land is a war for and against slavery; and that it can never be effectually put down till one or the other of these vital forces is completely destroyed."[3] As with his response to the Dred Scott decision, Douglass's words predicted the future: Slavery would become the main issue of the conflict. And by the time the war was over, blacks, slave and free, would play a significant part in the conflict.

Two

"Fighting the Rebels with One Hand," April 1861–April 1862

In some ways, the Confederate capture of Fort Sumter came as a relief for both sides. The tension between North and South had been agonizing; now, the battle lines had been drawn. On both sides, admirals and generals held war councils to plot strategy; factories geared up to produce war materials; forts were reinforced; horses and wagons were ordered into service; railroad cars were fitted out to carry men and supplies. Everyone thought the war would be brief, for both sides were certain that their cause was just and victory assured. In both the Union and Confederate armies, the initial length of enlistment was ninety days, and so the war was talked about as a "ninety-days' war." Blacks in both regions were eager to be part of it.

Blacks in the South, both slave and free, were skeptical of the intentions of all whites, whether Rebel or Yankee. Those blacks who lived far from the North were fed a steady diet of stories that northerners would treat them far worse than southerners treated them. Southern blacks who lived in closer contact with the North, or who were able to read, knew that although the worst stories were untrue, the North was no Promised Land, that free blacks in the North were denied many of the rights enjoyed by whites. A strong sense of realism borne of years of suffering led most southern blacks to make their decisions out of self-interest rather than any political theory or moral abstraction. During most of the war, the Unionist or Confederate sympathies of black southerners fluctuated with changing circumstances: When they had little hope of escaping their present conditions, they were loyal to the Confederacy. But when they saw an opportunity to improve their circumstances, they did not hesitate to switch their loyalty.

After the attack on Fort Sumter, when people across the South were certain that the Confederate States would easily establish their right to separate nationhood, many free people of color were staunchly loyal to their states. In New Orleans, where Louisiana's free people of color were concentrated, many of the men were sons and grandsons of Negroes who had distinguished themselves fighting the British in the Battle of New Orleans in 1815 and who had been praised for their efforts by General Andrew Jackson. Most of these men were wealthy property owners, some of them slave owners themselves, and they feared that Union forces would confiscate their property.

On April 21, 1861, 1,500 free people of color met to organize a regiment for the protection of the South, and especially of New Orleans, against the North, the "enemy." They organized themselves into a regiment of eight state militia companies, called the Louisiana Native Guards. However, the Native Guards were never called to combat. Soon after they were organized, a number of free blacks were found in Louisiana masquerading as slaves to avoid suspicion and traveling on slave passes. Mainly from the West, they were suspected of being sent as Union spies to learn all they could about military preparations in the South. The arrests of those free blacks as spies cast suspicion on all free people of color, and this may have been one reason why the Native Guards did not see action.

Not only in New Orleans, but elsewhere in the South, free blacks offered their services for combat in the hope of securing better treatment in return. But too many southerners distrusted their motives and feared the idea of arming black men.

Free blacks were not generally accepted into the Confederate military except as musicians. As in the Union military, drummers and fifers were not subject to the same regulations as regular soldiers, because their jobs were considered noncombat positions. Boys younger than the eligible age of eighteen, or shorter than the eligible height of five feet five inches, were routinely accepted into service as musicians. In reality, however, in battle they were in as much danger as the older men. The notes they played on their instruments served to identify the location of their regiments in the smoke and fury of battle, which made them prime targets for the enemy. Quite a number of free blacks later applied for govern-

A black cook at City Point, Virginia. After the Union forces began to accept blacks into their ranks, Negro enlistees were more likely to be employed as cooks, builders of fortifications, and in other support roles than as combatants. (Library of Congress)

ment pensions based on their service as musicians in the Confederate military.

Southern slaves were far more common on the battlefront than were free blacks. Slaves were the laborers of the South, and in wartime they continued to serve that function. From the beginning, the Confederacy used slave labor to build its fortifications, load its supplies, work on its railroads, staff its hospitals, perform veterinary tasks, cook meals, bury the dead, and do the other noncombat jobs that are required to keep an army going. Later on, they took over the jobs in light manufacturing that had been held by whites who enlisted or were drafted into the war. By using slave labor in these ways, the Confederate army freed its white men for combat. This tactic was essential, considering the comparative population of the Union and the Confederacy. The twenty-three states of the Union had a free population of 22 million, while the eleven Confederate states had a free population of only 6 million. Every third southerner was black, and the vast majority of blacks were slaves.

Still, a number of southern slaves wound up fighting on the Confederate side. In many cases, slave masters who enlisted in the Confederate forces brought along slaves as body servants to attend to their personal needs in camp. While these slaves were supposed to function in noncombat roles, Union bullets and cannonballs did not distinguish between combatants and noncombatants. Slaves who accompanied their masters to war often found themselves in the thick of fighting, and when they did, they were likely to fight back.

Three anecdotes, all from Virginia in 1861, serve to illustrate some of the ways in which southern slaves saw combat on the Confederate side.

The first is the story of a Georgia slave named Dave, who had accompanied his master to war and was with his owner in Virginia when he happened to see the horse belonging to his owner's commanding officer fall underneath the officer. Seeing a Yankee soldier raise his gun and take aim at the officer, Dave in turn raised his gun. The Yankee surrendered, and the recovered officer took him prisoner.

A second example of how blacks were involved in the war at this time is that of a Major Chichester, who lived near the Fairfax, Virginia, Courthouse. The major decided to enlist for combat, creating particular upheaval for the Wests, a slave family on his estate that included five boys and two girls. Chichester chose sixteen-year-old Daniel West to accompany him into military service as a body servant. To keep the estate operating, he chose to keep one West boy and one West girl in Virginia. The remaining three boys and one girl were to be sent to Mississippi.

Daniel West served the major throughout the war, later boasting to his grandchildren of the musket he carried to protect his master.

A third illustration of blacks in the war is shown in a report conveying information learned by scouts working for the Union forces stationed at Camp Butler in Virginia. The report attests to the use of blacks to man a Confederate howitzer battery in August 1861.

Camp Butler, Newport News, Virginia
August 11, 1861

Sir: Scouts from this post represent the enemy as having retired. They came to New Market Bridge on Wednesday and left the next day. They said the enemy talked of having nine thousand men. They were recalled by dispatches from Richmond. They had twenty pieces of artillery among which was the Richmond howitzer battery manned by Negroes.

I am, respectfully, your obedient servant, J. W. Phelps, Colonel Commanding.

Lieutenant Charles C. Churchill, Acting Assistant
Adjutant General, Fort Monroe, Virginia [1]

While the report does not specify whether the Negro gunners were slave or free, they were almost certainly slaves.

In the North, free blacks wanted to volunteer for military service because they believed that the war was being fought over slavery and understood that their own conditions would be improved if slavery were abolished. They also hoped to distinguish themselves in the fighting so that white northerners might look more favorably upon them. Life was no picnic for blacks in the North. Although slavery had been officially abolished in most northern states by 1830, blacks were segregated—if not by law then by custom. Blacks were routinely denied jobs and housing because of their color, were not permitted to enter many white restaurants and places of entertainment, suffered inferior schools, and were generally treated as second-class citizens. A 1797 federal law existed that barred black men from state militias, and although no law prevented them from serving in the United States Army, by custom that, too, was a white man's preserve.

Within five days after the attack on Fort Sumter, a black organization in Pittsburgh, Pennsylvania, called the Hannibal Guards, sent a letter to General James S. Negley, militia commander of Western Pennsylvania:

> Sir: As we sympathize with our white fellow-citizens at the present crisis, and to show that we can and do feel interested in the present state of affairs; and as we consider ourselves American citizens and interested in the Commonwealth of all our white fellow-citizens, although deprived of all our political rights, we yet wish the government of the United States to be sustained against the tyranny of slavery, and are willing to assist in any honorable way or manner to sustain the present Administration [Abraham Lincoln's presidency]. We therefore tender to the state the services of the Hannibal Guards.[2]

On April 23, a black man in the U.S. Congress, named Jacob Dobson, who was employed in the chambers of the United States, sent a note to Secretary of War Simon Cameron, advising the secretary, "Sir: I desire to inform you that I know of some three hundred of reliable colored free citizens of this City, who desire to enter the service for the defence of the City."[3]

Also on April 23, in Boston, Massachusetts, a group of black citizens met at the Twelfth Street Baptist Church to call for the repeal of laws preventing them from joining the state militia. A few days later, blacks in that city organized a military-style unit for the purpose of drilling, or practicing, military formations. In Cleveland, Ohio, as well as in Massachusetts, blacks petitioned the state legislature to repeal the laws preventing them from serving in the state militia. But there was no strong public support for black men in combat, and officials in both states did nothing.

Local officials not only did nothing to help black men serve, they actively denied Negroes the opportunity even to prepare for possible military duty. In New York City, a group of black men rented a hall, formed a military club, and began to drill in case they were called to serve. But the police stopped them, warning that there was no way to protect them from mob assault by the "lower classes" of the city, mostly Irish immigrants.

Blacks in Cincinnati, Ohio, a staunchly pro-slavery city, organized a Black Brigade. But they were rebuffed by police, who refused to allow one meeting in a schoolhouse and demanded that the owner of a business that served as a recruiting station take down the American flag he had placed above his door. The Black Brigade disbanded shortly thereafter. At another point, blacks held a meeting to form a company of "Home Guards", whose purpose would be to aid in the defense of the city in the event of attack. But the police shut down that effort as well, shouting, "We want you damned niggers to keep out of this; this is a white man's war."[4]

"A Negro Family coming into the Union Lines." This was one in a series of stereoscope cards about the Civil War produced after the war was over. The stereoscope was a popular form of home entertainment in the late nineteenth and early twentieth centuries. Invented in England in the 1830s, it was created for popular use after the development of photography in the 1840s. The principle of the stereoscope is the same as that of binoculars: Human eyes, being a certain distance apart, see slightly different aspects of a scene. A single photograph shows no more than one eye would see. For a stereoscope, two photographs are taken from positions related approximately to the positions of a person's two eyes. The person's brain combines the two images into a single, three-dimensional one. (Library of Congress)

Black volunteers were unwanted volunteers. From President Lincoln on down, the white northern view was that the war was about preserving the Union. It had nothing to do with blacks and was not about slavery. As a practical matter, Lincoln and Congress did not want to anger the four slaveholding border states—Delaware, Maryland, Kentucky, and Missouri—that had reluctantly remained in the Union after the Confederate attack on Fort Sumter, but were still firmly pro-slavery.

Most northern generals also saw the issues of slavery and preserving the Union as separate and refused to harbor escaped slaves who managed to reach Union encampments in the South. They also had practical reasons for this refusal, since the refugees would slow the movement of their troops and eat the food meant for the fighting forces. As a rule, at least in the early days of the war, Union generals returned the fugitives to the Confederates.

Such actions infuriated blacks. On May 9, 1861, the Reverend J. Sella Martin, pastor of the Joy Street Baptist Church, in Boston, wrote to Frederick Douglass in outrage about a letter he had received from Mobile, Alabama, reporting that A. J. Slemmer, a Union officer, had returned fugitives:

They refuse to let the white man sell the Southerners food,
and yet they return slaves to work on the plantation to raise
all the food that the Southerners want. They arrest traitors,
and yet make enemies of the colored people, North and South;
and if they do force the slave to fight for her master, as the
only hope of being benefited by the war, they may thank their
own cowardice and prejudice for the revenge of the negro's aid
and the retribution of his bullet while fighting against them
in the Southern States. I received a letter from Mobile, in
which the writer states that the returning of those slaves by
Slemmer has made the slaves determined to fight for the
South, in the hope that their masters may set them free after
the war, and when remonstrated with, they say that the North
will not let them fight for them. 5

A few Union generals departed from the norm. In late May 1861, the same month as the Reverend Martin wrote to Frederick Douglass to express his outrage over A. J. Slemmer's returning fugitive slaves to the Confederates, Union Major General Benjamin F. Butler took the opposite course from Slemmer.

On the night of May 23, 1861, three escaped slaves reached the Union outpost at Fortress Monroe, in Virginia, where Butler was in command. When the slaves' master contacted Butler and demanded their return, Butler refused. On learning that the slaves had been utilized in the building of Confederate fortifications, he declared them "contrabands of war", stated that he was not obligated to return property to a foreign government, and put the escaped slaves to work building fortifications for his troops, paying them wages for their efforts.

News of Butler's decision quickly spread throughout the region, and two days after the first three slaves sought his protection, eight more arrived at what the slaves had come to call "Freedom Fort." Another fifty-nine men and women showed up the following day, putting Butler in a quandary.

Major General Butler understood that he was venturing into new legal and political territory, and on May 27, 1861, he wrote to the general in chief of the army, explaining his feelings and asking for guidance:

> *As a matter of property to the insurgents* [sheltering the escaped slaves] *will be of very great moment, the number*

that I now have amounting as I am informed to what in good times would be of the value of sixty thousands dollars. Twelve of these negroes I am informed have escaped from the erection of the batteries on Sewall's Point which this morning fired upon my expedition as it passed by out of range. As a means of offense therefore in the enemy's hands these negroes when able-bodied are of the last importance. Without them the [Confedcrate] batteries could not have been erected at least for many weeks. As a military question it would seem to be a measure of necessity to deprive their masters of their services. How can this be done? As a political question and a question of humanity can I receive the services of a Father and a Mother and not take the children? Of the humanitarian aspect I have no doubt. Of the political one I have no right to judge. I therefore submit all this to your better judgment . . . [6]

President Lincoln agreed that Butler's policy of keeping "contrabands" was a legitimate tactic of war. Frederick Douglass approved as well, but noted that the term *contraband* was "a name that will apply better to a pistol, than to a person." Douglass insisted that when slaves were referred to they should be called persons, not things. [7]

Within two months, attitudes in the North toward using escaped southern slaves began to change even more, primarily because of events in the war. In July 1861, at the first Battle of Bull Run, at Manassas, Virginia, the first major battle of the war, thirty thousand Union troops were pushed back by a force of twenty-two thousand Confederate troops led by General Thomas "Stonewall" Jackson. The defeat at Bull Run was a great shock to the Yankees, who were suddenly forced to face the reality that the war would be neither short nor easy to win.

The South had many advantages in the war, not the least of which was that the theater of battle was in its own territory; the Confederate forces were fighting on their own ground. Another advantage was the strong military tradition among the slaveholding class, who had dominated the nation's military academies and military services before the war. Still another advantage was that, at least at first, the South did not see its mission as winning the war so much as protecting itself from Union invasion and conquest. But the greatest advantage enjoyed by the Rebel forces was its ability to employ thousands of slaves in the war effort. The North couldn't do much about the location of battles or the greater military experience of its enemy, but it could do something about the Confederate use of slaves.

Frederick Douglass wrote that the events at the first Battle of Bull Run had ". . . much changed the tone of Northern sentiment as to the proper mode of prosecuting the war, in reference to slavery, the cause of the war. Men now call not only for vengeance and righteous retribution, but for the destruction of the cause of their great national disaster. A cry has gone forth for the abolition of slavery. . . . If the defeat at Bull's Run shall have the effect to teach the Government this high wisdom, and to distinguish between its friends and foes at the South, that defeat, terrible as it is, will not have been entirely disastrous."[8]

On August 6, 1861, Congress passed a Confiscation Act, which gave the federal government authority to seize any property used to aid the rebellion and to free slaves working for the Confederacy. Passage of this legislation was, in part, an attempt to make General Butler's contraband policy more systematic, for some generals did not have the same humanitarian sense as Butler and were turning away all fugitive slaves who could not prove they had actively aided the Confederates. By October, Union generals were authorized to employ fugitive slaves in noncombat service, performing the same types of work that slaves were doing for the Confederacy, and to deal with feeding, clothing, and housing them in the best way they could.

The largest concentration of contraband was on the South Carolina Sea Islands off the state's coast. The Union army captured the island in late 1861. The plantation owners fled, leaving behind some ten thousand slaves. Word got around that the islands had been liberated, and slaves from all over the South made their way there. The runaways were in desperate straits—hungry and ill-clothed—and when word reached the North of their situation many northerners sent money, clothing, and medicine. Others traveled south to the Sea Islands to open schools for the illiterate slaves. These northern teachers included blacks and whites, among them Charlotte Forten, a black woman who came from a prominent

A group of about one hundred blacks, mostly children, in a mass reading class at "Freedman's Village" in Arlington, Virginia. Behind them are the barracks where they were housed. (Library of Congress)

Philadelphia abolitionist family.

In a report on her experiences published in the December 19, 1862, issue of *The Liberator*, a newspaper published by the white abolitionist William Lloyd Garrison, Forten told of how one former Sea Islands slave had remained behind after his master had fled the Union advance: "Harry says that his master told him that the Yankees would certainly shoot every one of them. 'Very well, massa', said he. 'If I go with you, I be as good as dead. So if I got to be dead, I believe I'll stay and wait for the Yankees'. He said he knew all the while there was no truth to what his master said." [9]

Thus far, the fugitive slaves were employed only as servants and construction workers. In November, Secretary of War Cameron went so far as to suggest that blacks be allowed to enlist in the Union army and navy. But the idea of arming blacks was still an outrage to many, especially in the slaveholding states that had remained loyal to the Union. An angry President Lincoln quashed Cameron's idea and removed him from his post two months later, in January 1862.

The following month, Union forces successfully routed the Confederates from Nashville, Tennessee, and seized that Confederate capital. Lincoln hoped that more Union victories would make it possible to avoid further action on slavery or further discussion of using blacks in combat. But in a speech that winter called "Fighting the Rebels with One Hand," Frederick Douglass charged, "We are striking the guilty rebels with our soft, white hand, when we should be striking with the iron hand of the black man."[10]

Three

"Men of Color, to Arms!" April 1862–April 1863

By April 1862, the Union army and the Union navy were working in concert to cut off strategic Confederate locations and supply lines on both land and sea. Early in the month, at the Battle of Shiloh, at Pittsburg Landing, in western Tennessee, Union troops commanded by General Ulysses S. Grant beat back Confederate forces in a bloody battle that left nearly four thousand men dead and more than sixteen

Union General Ulysses S. Grant at a field camp in July 1864. (Library of Congress)

thousand wounded. The Union victory at Shiloh, combined with the seizure of Nashville, Tennessee, two months earlier, in effect destroyed the Confederate defense of the western regions of the Confederacy.

In the meantime, the Union navy was doing its best to cut off the South's major seaports. After the northern loss at Bull Run in July 1861, President Lincoln had decided it was time to exploit the superior strength of the Union Navy. The North had two bases in the South: Hampton Roads, near Norfolk, Virginia, and Key West, Florida. Lincoln ordered increased efforts on the part of the navy to blockade the South's main ports and to seize them wherever possible.

One port that the Union navy managed to blockade effectively was Charleston, South Carolina, a situation that presented a slave named Robert Smalls with an opportunity to escape to the Union side.

Smalls and his brother, John, had been working, respectively, as assistant pilot and assistant engineer on the side-wheel steamer *Planter*, carrying goods in the harbor and inland waters, when the Civil War broke out. Like all other useful vessels, the *Planter* was pressed into service for the Confederate cause. Her main job was to carry supplies and munitions from the mainland out to Fort Ripley and Fort Sumter, which were prevented from receiving supplies by sea because of the Union blockade.

In the spring of 1862, Robert Smalls began to think seriously about hijacking the *Planter* and making a run for the Union blockade, even though two white Confederate naval officers were assigned to oversee the work of the Negro crew. He and his brother enlisted the

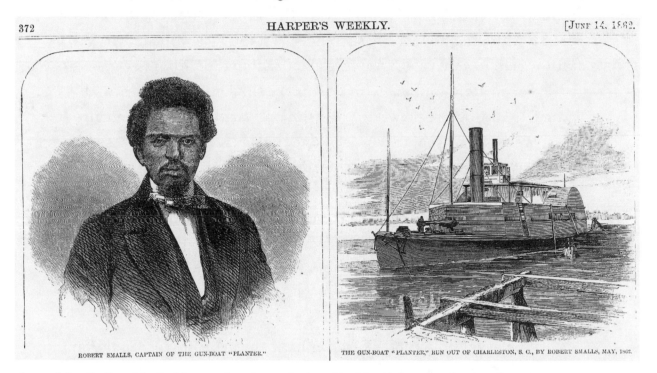

ROBERT SMALLS, CAPTAIN OF THE GUN-BOAT "PLANTER."

THE GUN-BOAT "PLANTER," RUN OUT OF CHARLESTON, S. C., BY ROBERT SMALLS, MAY, 1862.

Captain Robert Smalls and the Confederate gunboat Planter *that he and his fellow black crew members brought through the Union naval blockade of Charleston Harbor in June 1862. Smalls and his crew served the Union on the* Planter *for the remainder of the Civil War, once narrowly escaping recapture by the Confederates, but there is no evidence that they ever enlisted in the Union navy. (Library of Congress)* support of the other black members of the crew, and one night when the white officers went ashore, the crew cast off from the dock at Charleston and slowly steamed down the harbor. As the *Planter* passed Fort Sumter, she fired her guns in salute. Since it was not unusual to see the ship traveling about in the early morning hours, she aroused no suspicion. The *Planter* managed to get by all the Confederate fortifications without any problem. Having passed the lower batteries, the crew raised a white flag to indicate surrender, and the *Planter* made her way at full steam toward the Union ships blockading the harbor's entrance.

Fortunately for Smalls and his party, the Union sailors saw the white flag just before they started to fire on *Planter* and held their fire. They were surprised to see no one but blacks aboard. As the Confederate vessel came near the stern of the Union ship *Onward*, Robert Smalls stepped forward, took off his hat, and said, "Good morning, sir! I've brought you some of the old United States guns, sir!"[1]

The United States government had a standard offer of prize money for any Confederate ship captured by Union forces. Smalls and his crew received half the prize money for the *Planter* and were allowed to remain on the ship.

The navy had accepted black enlistees even before the Civil War

MEN OF COLOR, TO ARMS! NOW OR NEVER!

This is our Golden Moment. The Government of the United States calls for every Able-Bodied Colored Man to enter the Army for the THREE YEARS' SERVICE, and join in fighting the Battles of Liberty and the Union. A new era is open to us. For generations we have suffered under the horrors of slavery, outrage and wrong; our manhood has been denied, our citizenship blotted out, our souls seared and burned, our spirits cowed and crushed, and the hopes of the future of our race involved in doubts and darkness. But now the whole aspect of our relations to the white race is changed. Now therefore is our most precious moment. Let us Rush to Arms! **Fail Now and Our Race is Doomed** on this the soil of our birth. We must now awake, arise, or be forever fallen. If we value Liberty, if we wish to be free in this land, if we love our country, if we love our families, our children, our homes, we must strike NOW while the Country calls: must rise up in the dignity of our manhood, and show by our own right arms that we are worthy to be freemen. Our enemies have made the country believe that we are craven cowards, without soul, without manhood, without the spirit of soldiers. Shall we die with this stigma resting on our graves? Shall we leave this inheritance of shame to our children? No! A thousand times No! **We WILL Rise!** The alternative is upon us; let us rather die freemen than live to be slaves. What is life without liberty? We say that we have manhood—now is the time to prove it. A nation or a people that cannot fight may be pitied, but cannot be respected. If we would be regarded *Men*, if we would forever **SILENCE THE TONGUE OF CALUMNY,** of prejudice and hate; let us rise NOW and fly to arms! We have seen what **Valor and Heroism** our brothers displayed at **PORT HUDSON and at MILLIKEN'S BEND;** though they are just from the galling, poisoning grasp of slavery, they have startled the world by the most exalted heroism. If they have proved themselves heroes, can not we prove ourselves men? **ARE FREEMEN LESS BRAVE THAN SLAVES?** More than a Million White Men have left Comfortable Homes and joined the Armies of the Union to save their Country; cannot we leave ours, and swell the hosts of the Union, to save our liberties, vindicate our manhood, and deserve well of our Country?

MEN OF COLOR! All Races of Men—the Englishman, the Irishman, the Frenchman, the German, the American, have been called to assert their claim to freedom and a manly character, by an appeal to the sword. The day that has seen an enslaved race in arms, has, in all history, seen their last trial. We can now see that **OUR LAST OPPORTUNITY HAS COME!** If we are not lower in the scale of humanity than Englishmen, Irishmen, white Americans and other races, we can show it now.

MEN OF COLOR! BROTHERS and FATHERS! WE APPEAL TO YOU! By all your concern for yourselves and your liberties, by all your regard for God and Humanity, by all your desire for Citizenship and Equality before the law, by all your love for the Country, to stop at no subterfuges, listen to nothing that shall deter you from rallying for the Army. Come forward, and at once Enroll your Names for the **Three Years' Service. STRIKE NOW,** and you are henceforth and forever **FREEMEN!**

E. D. Bassett,
Wm. D. Forten,
Frederick Douglass,
Wm. Whipper,
D. D. Turner,
Jas. McCrummell,
A. S. Cassey,
A. M. Green,
J. W. Page,
L. R. Seymour,
Rev. J. Underdue,

John W. Price,
Augustus Dorsey,
Rev. Stephen Smith,
N. W. Depee,
Dr. J. H. Wilson,
J. W. Cassey,
P. J. Armstrong,
J. W. Simpson,
Rev. J B. Trusty,
S. Morgan Smith,
Wm. E. Gipson,

Rev. J. Boulden,
Rev. J. Asher,
Rev. J. C. Gibbs,
Daniel George,
Robert M. Adger,
Henry M. Cropper,
Rev. J. B. Reeve,
Rev. J. A. Williams,
Rev. A. L. Stanford,
Thomas J. Bowers,
Elijah J. Davis,

John P. Burr,
Robert Jones,
O. V. Catto,
Thos. J. Dorsey,
I. D. Cliff,
Jacob C. White,
Morris Hall,
James Needham,
Rev. Elisha Weaver,
Ebenezer Black,
Rev. Wm. T. Catto,

Jas. R. Gordon,
Samuel Stewart,
David B. Bowser,
Henry Minton,
Daniel Colley,
J. C. White, Jr.,
Rev. J. P. Campbell,
Rev. W. J. Alston,
J. P. Johnson,
Franklin Turner,
Jesse E. Glasgow.

"Men of Color, to Arms! Now or Never!" When at last the Union army agreed to accept black enlistments, Frederick Douglass and more than fifty other prominent leaders signed this recruitment poster enthusiastically urging African-American men to join the Union cause. (Library of Congress)

broke out, but there is no evidence that either Smalls or any of his crew actually enlisted or were commissioned in the United States Navy. There was always at least one white Union officer on board, for it was not navy policy to place blacks in command positions. Smalls and his crew served the Union on the *Planter* for the remainder of the Civil War, once narrowly escaping recapture by the Confederates.

Meanwhile, in the western Confederacy, Union Admiral David Farragut had, in February 1862, taken charge of a fleet of sloops and gunboats and headed down the Mississippi River toward New Orleans. By April 26, his fleet had captured two strategic forts on the river seventy-five miles below the city. Disregarding his orders to cease his attack after those victories, Farragut then captured the city.

Faced with the responsibility of controlling a hostile population deep inside the Confederacy, President Lincoln decided to take advantage of the large number of freeborn blacks in New Orleans and took the unprecedented step of allowing the enlistment of black troops. Major General Benjamin F. Butler, commander of the Department of the Gulf, then issued an order calling upon freeborn men of color in Louisiana to take up arms in defense of the Union.

Many of the men who had earlier offered their services to the

Confederate cause now did the same for the Union. Twenty-four-year-old Pinckney Benton Stewart Pinchback, son of a white planter and his mulatto slave, immediately offered to recruit a company and was authorized to do so. In just over a week, Pinchback managed to raise an entire company for the new Corps d'Afrique, as it was called in New Orleans. The Second Louisiana Native Guards entered into service for the Union on October 12, 1862, under the command of Captain P. B. S. Pinchback. The other officers of the regiment were also black.

It was an unprecedented move to allow black officers in that company and in the First Louisiana Native Guards, which was also composed of freemen of color. The general feeling about blacks on the part of Union commanders was that black soldiers could only be useful under the command of whites, and Major General Benjamin F. Butler's attitude was no different. But under pressure from Lincoln's administration and through military necessity, Butler accepted the black troops for service along with their black officers. The Third Louisiana Native Guards, which, unlike the other two regiments, was composed of escaped slaves, also had black officers.

While official Union government attitudes toward employing blacks in combat were changing, there was much disorganization and

Soldiers on review in South Carolina. Note that the officers, standing in front of the line of troops, are white. (Library of Congress)

confusion over policy during the spring and summer of 1862. In May, General David Hunter, commander of the Department of the South, which included Georgia, Florida, and South Carolina, issued an order freeing all slaves in those states and began recruiting ex-slaves from the Sea Islands off South Carolina for the first regiment of South Carolina Volunteers. An angry President Lincoln declared that General Hunter had exceeded his authority, disavowed the general's Emancipation Proclamation, and ordered the First South Carolina Colored Volunteer Regiment disbanded.

Just three months later, on August 25, 1862, the War Department authorized General Rufus Saxton, military governor of the South Carolina Sea Islands, to organize five regiments of black troops on the islands. By early November, the first regiment had been mustered: the First South Carolina Volunteer Infantry under the command of Colonel Thomas Wentworth Higginson. Higginson, a Massachusetts abolitionist, had no doubt of the bravery of his men, noting, "There were more than a hundred men in the ranks who had voluntarily met more dangers in their escape from slavery than any of my young captains had incurred in their lives."[2]

But in most other cases, the president declined to recognize black units. In August, James Lane, a Kansas senator and a general in the state militia, who was also a staunch abolitionist regarded as an outlaw and a renegade by some, organized the First Kansas Colored Volunteer Regiment, over the opposition of Secretary of War Edwin Stanton. The regiment, which was made up of ex-slaves from Arkansas, Kansas, Missouri, and the Indian Territory, wore nonregulation uniforms but had the distinction of being the first black unit to engage the enemy. In late October 1862, several months before it was officially mustered into the Union army, the unit saw action against a unit of Confederate guerrillas at Island Mounds, Missouri. One member of the First Kansas was killed in that skirmish, the first black to die in combat on the side of the Union.

Two regiments of black men organized in Indiana in early August were also denied recognition.

By the late summer of 1862, the Confederacy was clearly ahead in the war. Except for the capture of Nashville, Tennessee, and Admiral Farragut's big naval victory at New Orleans, the Union had consistently been frustrated in its attempts to rout the Confederate forces. The war's chief battleground had continued to be Virginia, dangerously close to both the federal capital of Washington, D.C., and the Confederate cap-

General Robert E. Lee, seated, flanked by Walter Taylor, left, and George Washington Custis Lee. This photograph was taken in Richmond, Virginia, after the war was over by Mathew B. Brady. Brady was authorized by President Lincoln to organize a photographic corps to accompany the Union troops; thanks to the huge visual record of the war this corps produced, the Civil War was the first war to be so thoroughly documented. (Library of Congress)

ital at Richmond, Virginia. Confederate strength in the Seven Days' Battle at Richmond in July had prompted Union General George B. McClellan to order his troops into retreat (although many in the government believed that McClellan, a strong advocate of slavery and an indecisive military strategist, need not have taken such a radical step). The Confederacy had also come out ahead in the second Battle of Bull Run in August, leading General Robert E. Lee, commander of the Confederate army in Virginia, to believe the way was open to invade the North.

The North was in a panic over this turn of events. More and more northerners began to believe that the single most important factor in the Confederates' strength was their use of slaves. As a result, more northerners turned against slavery. In July 1862, Congress passed two acts providing for the enlistment of Negro soldiers. The first, the Confiscation Act, authorized the president to employ "as many persons of African descent as he may deem necessary" to suppress the rebellion. The second, the Militia Act, repealed the provisions of a 1792 law barring black men from serving in state militia and authorized the employment of free Negroes (born free) and freedmen (those who had been granted or who had purchased their freedom) as soldiers.

In August, the War Department, in a radical shift in policy, issued a statement that henceforth all slaves admitted into military service were declared free, along with their wives and children.

President Lincoln had been forced to alter his objectives in the war. He could no longer focus on preserving the Union; to win the war, he would have to destroy the Confederacy. To do that, he believed, he would have to emancipate, or free, the slaves held in bondage by the Confederate states. He considered it not so much a humanitarian gesture as a military tactic—a psychological blow to the Confederacy.

He had another reason to free the Confederate slaves: He believed it would help prevent the Confederacy from receiving international recognition as a separate nation. Since its founding, the Confederacy had sought official recognition as a separate nation by the rest of the world. In particular, the Confederacy wanted diplomatic recognition from England and France, which were major markets for the South's cotton and tobacco exports. Also, the Confederacy believed that official recognition from Europe would help influence the Union to accept its status as a separate nation.

Concerned that England and France were indeed considering official recognition of the Confederate States of America, President

Lincoln decided to exploit the Confederacy's greatest weakness in the eyes of the Europeans: slavery. Especially to the European working classes, slavery and the aristocratic traditions of southern slaveholders were a great evil. But Lincoln realized he could not exploit that hatred unless the Union took a firm stand against slavery.

Lincoln's secretary of war, Edwin Stanton, urged the president not to issue the emancipation order while the North was faring poorly in the war but to wait for a clear Union victory, after which he could make the announcement from a position of strength.

That victory came in September, when Confederate General Robert E. Lee, frustrated with a war that he always had to conduct on the defensive, decided to take the offensive and attempted to invade Maryland, launching the attack at Antietam.

The Battle of Antietam was one of the bloodiest yet, with thousands of casualties on both sides (nearly five thousand on the battlefield; another three thousand men died as a result of the wounds they suffered in the battle). Despite severe losses, Union forces managed to drive the Confederates from Maryland. While the battle raged, President Lincoln prayed for a victory. When it came, he wasted little time in deploying his new military tactic.

Five days after the Union victory at Antietam, the president announced that he would issue an Emancipation Proclamation, freeing the slaves in the Confederate states as of January 1, 1863.

The proclamation, presented to Congress in draft form in the fall of 1862, freed only the slaves in the Confederacy because by law that's all Lincoln could do. Slaves were Confederate property, and it was his right as commander in chief of the Union forces to order the seizure of enemy property. He could not do the same for slaves in the Union because the president had no constitutional right to act against slavery there. Thus, slaves remained in bondage in the slaveholding states that had stayed loyal to the Union, and the Confederate states lost the very right that they had seceded from the Union to protect.

Confederates reacted predictably to the draft proclamation, refusing to be bound by it and declaring that it was not worth the paper it was written on. On October 10, Confederate President Jefferson Davis issued a call to the state of Virginia to draft 4,500 slaves to build fortifications around Richmond.

But blacks across the land rejoiced. In the South, those who could read were able to learn of the draft proclamation in southern newspapers. In New Orleans, the editor of the journal *L'Union*, founded by free blacks in 1862, proclaimed in the paper's December 6, 1862, issue, "Men of my blood! Shake off the contempt of your proud oppressors. Enough of shame and submission; the break is complete! Down with the craven behavior of bondage! Stand up under the noble flag of the Union and declare yourselves noble champions of the right. Defend your rights against the barbarous and imbecile spirit of slavery . . ." [3]

Other southern blacks learned of the Emancipation Proclamation through the efficient slave grapevine; but some acted as if responding to the call of the journal *L'Union*. In an area of Virginia north of Richmond, a slave named James Henry Woodson, father of Carter G. Woodson, the noted African-American historian, had been hired out by his owner to a ditchdigger named James Stratton. Stratton frequently whipped Woodson. One day, Woodson whipped Stratton back, crying that he was free (he'd heard about the Emancipation Proclamation) and did not have to take that treatment. Woodson then ran away and sought refuge with a Union cavalry detachment, to which he provided valuable information about where the cavalry could get supplies, acting as a guide for them.

Up in the North, most blacks saved their celebrations until President Lincoln actually signed the Emancipation Proclamation on

President Abraham Lincoln assembled his Cabinet for a first reading of the Emancipation Proclamation in the fall of 1862. Although the document did not take effect until January 1, 1863, world quickly spread throughout the country and African Americans, slave and free, rejoiced. (Library of Congress)

January 1, 1863. In Boston, Frederick Douglass and some six thousand other blacks held an all-day vigil, waiting first for news that the president had signed the document and then for the actual text to be telegraphed to the local telegraph office. When the words of the telegram were read to the assembled crowd—"I do order and declare that all persons held as slaves within said designated States and parts of States are, and henceforward shall be, free . . ."—the crowd went wild. Recalled Douglass, "I never saw Joy before. Men, women, young, and old, were up; hats and bonnets were in the air."[4]

Douglass was especially excited over a provision in the formal Emancipation Proclamation providing that henceforth freed slaves "of suitable condition" would be "received into the armed service of the United States, to garrison forts, positions, stations, and other places, and to man vessels of all sorts in said service." Douglass had long pressed for black enlistment, arguing that blacks should have the right to fight for their own cause. He believed that if President Lincoln was willing to enlist former slaves in the Union forces, then the government might also accept the enlistment of free blacks. In the words of Douglass's biographer William S. McFeely, "Douglass all but snatched the Emancipation Proclamation from Abraham Lincoln's hands to make of its flat rhetoric a sharpened call for freedom and equality . . . . For Douglass, each gain in the struggle, and the Emancipation Proclamation decidedly was one of the greatest gains, simply meant that America must move on to the next step—right away. No one, including President Lincoln, would be allowed to rest on his laurels." [5]

Douglass again called on black men to enlist and "smite with death the power that would bury the Government and your liberty in the same hopeless grave." [6]

Secretary of War Edwin M. Stanton now began to authorize the organization of colored regiments. Such authorization was granted to Governor John A. Andrew, of Massachusetts, in January 1863. Although Andrew sought permission to recruit and organize black soldiers, there was no question that a white officer would command this regiment, and finding that white officer was one of Andrew's first orders of business. The governor had just the officer in mind: Colonel Robert Gould Shaw, Virginia-born son of abolitionists who had commanded the Second Massachusetts Infantry Regiment. Although he was concerned that he would be subject to ridicule for commanding a black regiment, Shaw accepted Andrew's offer, receiving a promotion to colonel.

Meanwhile, Andrew appointed recruiters to raise the regiment. The following ad ran in Boston newspapers in February:

TO COLORED MEN

Wanted. Good men for the Fifty-Fourth Regiment of Massachusetts. Volunteers of African descent, Col. Robert G. Shaw (commanding). $100 bounty [reward] at expiration of term of service. Pay $13 per month, and State aid for families. All necessary information can be obtained at the office, corner Cambridge and North Russell Streets.

Lieut. J. W. M. Appleton
Recruiting Officer [7]

Frederick Douglass and other noted abolitionists traveled to Boston to speak at black churches to urge enlistment. Douglass also published an editorial in his newspaper *Douglass' Monthly*:

MEN OF COLOR, TO ARMS!

When first the rebel cannon shattered the walls of Sumter and drove away its starving garrison, I predicted that the war then and there inaugurated would not be fought out entirely by white men . . . A war undertaken and brazenly carried on for the perpetual enslavement of colored men, calls logically and loudly for colored men to help suppress it . . . Go quickly and help fill up the first colored regiment from the North. I am authorized to assure you that you will receive the same wages, the same rations, the same equipments, the same protection, the same treatment, and the same bounty, secured to white soldiers.[8]

HARPER'S WEEKLY.
A JOURNAL OF CIVILIZATION.

Vol. VII.—No. 324.]   NEW YORK, SATURDAY, MARCH 14, 1863.   [SINGLE COPIES SIX CENTS.
[$3.00 PER YEAR IN ADVANCE.

Entered according to Act of Congress, in the Year 1863, by Harper & Brothers, in the Clerk's Office of the District Court for the Southern District of New York.

TEACHING THE NEGRO RECRUITS THE USE OF THE MINIE RIFLE.—[SEE PAGE 175.]

"Teaching the Negro Recruits the Use of the Minie Rifle," Harper's Weekly, *March 14, 1863. Although government authorities finally allowed the recruitment of black men to help the Union cause, they refused to accept blacks as commissioned officers. White officers commanded the Negro regiments, usually unhappily, because of the deep prejudice of most whites against blacks. (Library of Congress)*

The recruitment ads and Douglass's editorial neglected to mention that black soldiers faced special risks in going to battle against the Confederacy. In January 1863, eleven days after the Emancipation Proclamation was issued, Confederate President Jefferson Davis had issued a proclamation of his own, stating that all black Union soldiers were outlaws and declaring that all escaped slaves "if captured in arms be at once delivered over to the executive authorities of the respective States to which they belong, to be dealt with according to the laws of said States." [9]

These laws provided that any black person, slave or free, found with a weapon be put to death, and Davis's proclamation would be interpreted by Confederate soldiers as a license to murder black Union soldiers.

Douglass's editorial was also misleading in promising equal treatment for black soldiers, but he did not know at the time what hardships they would face and what unequal treatment they would suffer. His article was reprinted throughout the North, where attempts were being made in many states to raise black regiments. Douglass himself traveled widely, lending his support to recruitment efforts, sometimes personally signing up two dozen or so men. Among the recruits for whom he was responsible were his sons Charles, nineteen, and Lewis, twenty-two.

Because Governor Andrew wanted his regiment to be a model one, he ordered very stringent physical examinations. One-third of the volunteers were rejected because of various ailments and physical conditions. Those who passed constituted an unusually strong and healthy group. They numbered one thousand men and made up ten companies (the lowest unit, commanded by a captain) in the regiment. They were primarily laborers and farmers, the majority in their twenties. Their educational level was higher than in many white regiments; only two could not read or write. They came from twenty-two states, the District of Columbia, Nova Scotia, and the West Indies, some traveling long distances for the opportunity to serve in a formally established black Union regiment. On a campground outside of Boston, they practiced becoming a unit, drilled, and prepared for battle.

Not only the regimental commander, Colonel Robert Gould Shaw, but also the assistant commander and the company commanders were white, most of them from abolitionist families. Governor Andrew wrote to Secretary of War Stanton noting that while the law did prohibit colored officers in white regiments, it did not prohibit "Colored officers in colored regiments" and asked if there could be some black line officers, surgeons, and a chaplain. But both Stanton and President Lincoln worried that the appointment of colored officers would further enrage those whites who already saw the enlistment of black soldiers as the first step toward racial equality. The average white northerner was against slavery in principle, but certainly had no interest in blacks having equal rights of citizenship. So Andrew's request was refused, and all twenty-nine officers were white.

The Fifty-fourth Massachusetts, an all-black regiment with white officers, was mustered into service in March 1863. Late in the same month, the secretary of war issued an order directing Adjutant General Lorenzo Thomas to organize black regiments in the Mississippi Valley. The Union was now moving quickly to enlist the help of blacks in the fight to preserve the Union.

Four

"By Arming the Negro We Have Added a Powerful Ally": April 1863–April 1864

By the beginning of the war's third year, southern life had been severely disrupted. Thousands of slaves had already escaped, thousands more would become fugitives. It is estimated that as many as five hundred thousand southern slaves became fugitives during the four years of the Civil War. The great majority of them lived in the

Confederate states along the Atlantic coast and the Mississippi River. Most of the battles of the war took place in those states, and the presence of Union forces was a strong incentive for slaves who sought their freedom.

As Louisiana and Mississippi became more vulnerable to invading Union forces, the roads to Texas were crowded with planters moving their slaves away from the Yankees. This forced migration was sometimes called "running the niggers." It tore black families apart, and dislocated people from the communities where they had been born and raised.

Although the so-called twenty-slave rule exempted owners of large numbers of slaves from serving in the Confederate military, many wealthy planters believed it was their patriotic duty to enlist and did so, leaving their plantations in the hands of sons, wives, or overseers who did not have the same control over the slaves as the masters had established. Familiar routines broke down, and discipline was weakened. Before the war, most runaways had been men, but now whole families decided that reaching freedom was worth the risk of capture.

By the third year of the war, disruptions in agricultural production, combined with Union blockades of key southern ports and the vast needs of the fighting forces, had caused severe food short-ages in the major southern cities. On April 2, a group of white Richmond, Virginia, women, mostly the wives of ironworkers, marched on the governor's mansion demanding food. The protest soon turned into a riot, which ended only when President Jefferson Davis threatened to have troops open fire on the women. That spring there were similar food riots in Atlanta and in Macon, Georgia, and in several other cities in Georgia and South Carolina. In the rural areas, although food shortages were not as severe, there was also growing discontent. Especially in the upper South, where most of the war's battles were fought, there was much destruction of small farms. The farmers in the region were not major slaveholders, and as time went on they began to feel that they were bearing the brunt of the war, while the wealthy land and slave owners of the lower South, for whom they felt the war was being fought, were not bearing their share of suffering. Although some hungry urbanites and resentful small farmers began to question the wisdom of continuing the war, most southerners remained loyal to the Confederate cause and were determined to see victory.

Despite the disruptions the war had caused, the South still

occupied a position of strength. The North, for all its seeming advantages in population, manufacturing capability, and naval strength, had not turned those advantages into victory. As the third year of the Civil War began, according to one estimate, the Union's Army of the Potomac had spent a total of only one month in actual battle.[1] Major battles had been separated by long months of inactivity. By tradition, both sides took the winter months off, their armies waiting out the bad weather in semipermanent winter camps. But during the weeks of fighting, the Union had thus far pursued the war in a persistently disorganized fashion that indicated both a lack of experience on the part of many of its officers and confusion on the part of its leaders as to just what their goals were.

By April 1863, the two sides were in a virtual stalemate. While the Union navy had seized the port of New Orleans and managed to blockade the port of Charleston, and while the Union army had captured Nashville, Tennessee, Confederate troops had scored an important victory at Fredericksburg, Maryland. Confederate cavalry had cut Union supply lines to the west, dashing Union hopes of seizing the strategic river town of Vicksburg, Mississippi. In May, the Confederates gained the advantage when, at Chancellorsville, Virginia, General Robert E.

Lee's armies beat back a Union force twice its size and then prepared to invade Pennsylvania.

By that same month, the War Department had decided it needed a separate bureau to handle the black military units. The Bureau of Colored Troops was established to direct the recruitment, organization, and service of the newly organized black troops. Meanwhile, the authorized black units began to see action.

In early April 1863, the Second Louisiana Native Guards went to Pascagoula, Mississippi, to disrupt a Confederate base of supply and operations and prevent troops in Mobile, Alabama, from

A series of three paintings entitled "War Episodes" by Thomas Waterman (1823-1903): "The Contraband," "The Volunteer," and "The Veteran." (Metropolitan Museum of Art)

going to Charleston, South Carolina. The 180 black troops and officers immediately found themselves under attack by Confederate forces, and they fought back during a four-hour battle. Two men were killed and eight wounded, while claiming twenty Confederate casualties. Union commander Colonel Nathan W. Daniels reported to his superiors that the men of the Second Louisiana Native Guards had shown great bravery. On May 18, the First Kansas Colored Volunteer Regiment, under the command of Colonel James M. Williams, saw action against the Confederates at Sherwood, Missouri. But the black troops had to be involved in more than skirmishes to prove their suitability for combat.

On the same day as the battle at Sherwood, Missouri, the Fifty-fourth Massachusetts Regiment received the regimental flags it would carry into battle. Immediately after the presentation of the flags, Colonel Robert Gould Shaw was ordered to report to General David Hunter in Hilton Head, South Carolina. Ten days later the troops boarded the ship *De Molay* for the South.

Barely had the Fifty-fourth Massachusetts made camp when Colonel James Montgomery ordered eight of the ten regiments to travel farther south to the vicinity of Darien, Georgia. They watched as Union gunboats fired on the town and then were ordered to plunder and torch the houses. Shaw protested, but Montgomery was determined to see his orders carried out. The men of the Fifty-fourth Regiment were ashamed that their first action was more like piracy

"Marching On!—The Fifty-fourth Massachusetts Colored Regiment Singing John Brown's March in the Streets of Charleston, February 21, 1865," Harper's Weekly, *March 18, 1865. Black Americans revered the martyred white abolitionist and paid tribute to his memory as they marched victoriously into the strategic southern port that Union forces had at last managed to capture. Within a month, the Confederacy had surrendered. (Library of Congress)*

than warfare. General Hunter, Montgomery's superior, lost his job as a result.

On June 30, when the regiment was mustered for pay for the first time, the men of the Fifty-fourth learned that they were not, after all, to receive equal pay with white soldiers. Instead of thirteen dollars plus a clothing allowance, they were to be given ten dollars, the rate given to laborers, minus three dollars for clothing that would be provided. Furious at this unequal treatment, they refused to accept the lower pay.

Governor Andrew was mortified by this slap in the face of his black troops. He offered to make up the difference with money from the state treasury. But the men of the Fifty-fourth refused. It was not the money but the principle involved. They believed that their federal government should pay them as much as white soldiers. Out of pride, they continued to refuse any pay at all for eighteen months, in spite of the hardships that decision imposed on their families. But they did not refuse to serve, although Shaw felt they should be released from duty if they were not to be treated equally with white troops.

Between May and June of that year, in the long and protracted battle of Port Hudson, Louisiana, Union forces included two Louisiana

Native Guard regiments and six Corps d'Afrique regiments. The two Native Guard regiments were the Third, which unlike the First and Second was made up of escaped slaves, and the First.

In the ranks of the First Louisiana Native Guards was sixteen-year-old Lieutenant John H. Crowder, who may have been the youngest officer in the Union army. Crowder had lied about his age when he had enlisted in the Native Guards, because he had wanted to serve his country and because he needed the military pay to support his mother. Born of free black parents, Crowder had managed with the help of a clergyman friend to become quite well-educated. He was also very mature for his age and committed to doing a good job. He earned the rank of lieutenant because of his efficiency and leadership qualities; but his youth, and possibly his pride, put off his fellow black officers. Crowder once asked his mother in a letter, "If *Abraham Lincoln* knew that a colored Lad of my age could command a company, what would he say [?]" [2]

Crowder looked forward to showing that black soldiers were capable in battle, and he got his chance the following month in the Battle of Port Hudson.

The Union plan was to mount an assault on the Louisiana

port, one of the three remaining positions on the Mississippi River still under Confederate control. Under the command of Major General Nathaniel P. Banks, the more than one thousand black soldiers were just one contingent in a giant horseshoe-shaped line of Union troops surrounding the well-fortified position of the more than six thousand Confederate troops. The black troops were at one end of the horseshoe, close to the river.

To get at the Confederates in this area, it was necessary either to wade through deep backwater or to cross a pontoon bridge not far from a bluff where Confederate sharpshooters were stationed with rifles to pick off enemy advancers. On the morning of May 27, 1863, the First Louisiana Native Guards began to cross the bridge and were immediately met with rifle fire. They pressed on. Some of the troops tried to wade through the backwater, while others tried to scale the bluff and pick off the riflemen. But a hail of Confederate bullets cut them down.

The black regiments had hoped for some support from white troops, as well as artillery fire. But the two artillery guns were quickly destroyed, and the white troops never materialized. Nevertheless, once the First Louisiana Native Guards had been scattered, the Third

Louisiana Native Guards stepped in, and were in turn mowed down by Confederate artillery and rifle fire.

Meanwhile, the white troops elsewhere in the horseshoe line were having no better success. After several more attempts to charge the Confederate position, the Union army retreated. The Confederate position was too strong and too well-fortified.

Nearly 200 black troops, some twenty percent of the black forces, had been killed or injured, including a number of young black officers of the First Louisiana Native Guards, who represented the best and the brightest of New Orleans's free blacks. Among them was young Lieutenant John H. Crowder. Critically wounded, he had been carried to the rear for treatment, but died that same day.

Many a story of unusual heroism on the part of the black troops came out of this battle. One concerns efforts to help the white Union General H. E. Paine, who on June 14 was severely wounded while far in advance and left on the ground while his troops were driven back several hundred yards. The adjutant general called for volunteers to go back and bring the general off the field; but even after the adjutant general offered a reward, no one volunteered to venture out on the wide-open plain which was swept with constant artillery fire.

Finally, a small squad of men from the Corps d'Afrique stepped forward. They explained that they realized many would die in the war before their people would get freedom, and that it might as well be them as anybody else. The sixteen volunteers then formed themselves into four groups. The first group of four set out with a stretcher and supplies of water and medicine. They had not gone fifty yards before one man went down; his companions pressed forward, but one by one they, too, went down. Without hesitation, the second group of four loaded up with supplies, started out on the field, and were also struck down. The third group fared better. Two of them were wounded, but the remaining two managed to reach the general. Although they were unable to bring General Paine off the field, they remained with him and aided him as best they could until evening, when other soldiers helped to carry him back to camp.[3]

Officers, white and black, had stories to tell of wounded black soldiers rejoining the fray rather than going to a field hospital, or of fighting on despite severe injuries. These officers also reported on the troops' exceptional determination to keep advancing when they knew they were certain to be assaulted by enemy fire. Major General Banks reported on his black troops: "The severe test to which they were subjected, and the determined manner in which they encountered the enemy, leaves upon my mind no doubt of their ultimate success."[4]

Ironically, Banks's own experience of the valor of the black soldiers did not change his disapproving attitude toward black officers. Banks had taken over as commander of the region after a brief stint by Major General Butler, who had accepted the Louisiana Native Guards complete with black officers. By the time of the Port Hudson battle, Banks had rid the Third Louisiana Native Guards of all their black officers. The First Louisiana Native Guards were a different story, for like the Second Louisiana Native Guards they were free blacks who resisted the pressure to replace their black officers with whites.

Resist though they might, the black officers and their troops were eventually forced to bow to the racism of the high command. One by one, they were disqualified and discharged, and white officers were brought in to take their places. Only P B S Pinchback was found qualified—because he was literate, or very light-complected, or both. He was one of the few blacks to attain the rank of captain during the Civil War.

But Pinchback encountered extreme prejudice from the white officers, who treated him little better than the black troops they commanded. By September 1863, he'd had enough. He wrote the following letter to Major General Banks:

> *Fort Pike, Louisiana, September 10, 1863*
> *General:*
> *In the organization of the regiment I am attached to (Twentieth Corps d'Afrique) I find nearly all the officers inimical to me, and I can foresee nothing but dissatisfaction and discontent, which will make my position very disagreeable indeed. I would therefore, respectfully tender my resignation, as I am confident by so doing I best serve the interest of the regiment.*
> *I have the honor to be, sir, very respectfully, your obedient servant.*
> *P. B. S. Pinchback*
> *Captain Second Class*
> *Louisiana National Guard* [5]

By the spring of 1863, the Union had finally committed to all-out war and had decided on a strategy of invading the South and capturing major strategic points. In May, General William Tecumseh Sherman began a march southward that, it was hoped, would end at Atlanta, Georgia, and the capture of that major Confederate city. There were no blacks among Sherman's troops.

There were also no organized black units at the Battle of Gettysburg, a major battle that was fought between July 1 and 3, 1863. In fact, there were probably more blacks in the Confederate forces, as body servants, teamsters, and the like, than in the Union forces. Among the blacks on the Confederate side was Daniel West, the Virginia slave who had accompanied his master, Major Chichester, when the major had enlisted back in 1861. Unbeknownst to Daniel West, his brother, Henry West, was with the opposing Union forces. Henry, who was to have been sent to Mississippi on the major's orders when the major left the plantation, had instead run away and made his way to Connecticut via the Underground Railroad and later enlisted in the Connecticut militia. In this battle, Union forces were successful in beating back a major invasion of the North by Confederate General Robert E. Lee. Lee's forces suffered incredible casualties—four thousand dead and another twenty-four thousand wounded or missing.

Almost simultaneously, on the western front, troops under the command of General Ulysses S. Grant captured the Confederate city of Vicksburg, Mississippi. Some thirty thousand Confederate soldiers surrendered to the Union troops at Vicksburg. Union victories at Port Hudson and Milliken's Bend, in which African-American soldiers had fought in substantial numbers, had helped make possible Grant's success at Vicksburg, a crucial victory that gave the Union control of the Mississippi Valley, the heart of the Confederacy and the region's richest agricultural area.

Despite these major Union victories, the war was far from over. The North still needed fresh recruits to its forces. Back in March 1863, Congress had passed a new Conscription Act, aimed at securing troops for the Union cause. The act was scheduled to take effect in July 1863. When July came, neither the Congress nor the President felt that the recent Union victories justified repealing the act, and allowed it to take effect.

The act provided for all able-bodied men, age twenty to forty-five, to be selected for three years of military service by an impartial lottery; but it also allowed an individual to pay the government three hundred dollars in place of serving, or to pay a substitute to take his place. For the average northern laborer, three hundred dollars was a year's salary. Many laborers in the North were recent immigrants, for the North had encouraged immigration during the war years in order to supply laborers to take the places of men who went to war. When the Conscription Act went into effect in July 1863, there were riots in cities across the North. In New York City, where the insult of the Conscription Act was added to the injury of rampant inflation, the rioting turned to murder. Immigrant laborers, many of them poor and unskilled Irish Catholics, seized the Second Avenue Armory containing rifles and ammunition, and attacked anyone they considered responsible for their woes—Protestant missionaries, draft officials, and wealthy businessmen. But their main target was the most vulnerable— the small black population of the city.

Tensions between African Americans and the immigrant population in the city had long been close to the boiling point, as the two groups competed for jobs and social standing. Irish immigrants were discriminated against nearly as much as blacks—some job advertisements warned "No Dogs or Irish Need Apply." Irish and African Americans competed for the lowest unskilled jobs, and lived in close proximity to one another in the worst areas in the city. For the immigrants, the Conscription Act was a government attempt to force them to serve in a war for the freedom of a people they despised.

The rioters murdered at least a dozen blacks and burned to the ground the city's Colored Orphan Asylum. Only when Union troops, including New York's Irish Brigade, were called back to the city to restore order was the rioting put down. Although it was small comfort to the families of the black victims of the riots, public opinion in the North became much more sympathetic to blacks as a result of the tragedy of the draft riots.

Meanwhile, the newly organized black units continued to fight the war. On the western front, the First Kansas Colored Volunteer Regiment saw action at Sherwood, Missouri, on May 18, 1863; in Indian Territory on July 1, 2, and 17, 1863; and in Lawrence, Kansas, on July 27, 1863.

On the eastern front, the Fifty-fourth Massachusetts Regiment finally saw real wartime action; and its assault on Fort Wagner, South Carolina, would make the regiment famous. On July 18, 1863, after a forced march that had lasted a day and a half, the men of the Fifty-fourth Massachusetts were called on to prove their mettle. Their mission was to capture Fort Wagner, a Confederate stronghold guarding the entrance to Charleston Harbor. They had only rested from their long march about thirty minutes when Brigadier General George C. Strong, who had replaced Colonel Montgomery, gave the order for the charge. The column advanced, and were immediately met by fire— from the fort's big guns as well as from muskets. Colonel Robert Gould Shaw was killed at the head of his regiment, but his men fought on. Many of them reached the fort's walls and clambered over them, aiming to disable the big guns. But the musket fire increased, and they were forced back. White regiments in the vicinity were supposed to support the Fifty-fourth, but for various reasons none were able to do so, and without that support the regiment finally had to retreat, having lost one-third of its men.

In the thick of the fighting, Sergeant William H. Carney saw the bearer of the American flag fall and grabbed the flag before it touched the ground. He planted it on the fort, taking Confederate bullets in each leg, one in the chest, and one in his right arm in the process. Just then the order came to retreat, and Carney picked up the flag again and carried it safely back to the Union lines, proud that "The old flag never touched the ground, boys."[6]

Although the Fifty-fourth's assault on Fort Wagner failed because it did not capture the fort, it proved the bravery of the men of the reg-

Men of the First New York Engineers and members of the Massachusetts Fifty-fourth Regiment working to build barriers against Confederate fire at Fort Wagner. (Massachusetts Commandery, Military Order of the Loyal Legion and the U. S. Army Military History Institute)

iment and their willingness to die for the Union cause. The men who had survived the assault knew this. Frederick Douglass's son Lewis wrote to his sweetheart Helen Amelia Loguen, the daughter of Douglass's friend and fellow abolitionist, the Reverend Jarmain Loguen: "This regiment has established its reputation as a fighting regiment not a man flinched, though it was a trying time. Men fell all around me. A shell would explode and clear a space of twenty feet, our men would close up again, but it was no use we had to retreat, which was a very hazardous undertaking. How I got out of that fight alive I cannot tell, but I am here. My Dear girl I hope again to see you. I must bid you farewell should I be killed. Remember if I die I die in a good cause. I wish we had a hundred thousand colored troops we would put an end to this war." [7]

Lewis Douglass survived the war and later married Helen Amelia Loguen.

Northern newspapers made much of the battle and of the bravery of the black troops. Union General Ulysses S. Grant, commander of all army forces, wrote to President Lincoln, "By arming the negro we have added a powerful ally. They will make good soldiers and taking them from the enemy weakens him in the same proportion they strengthen us. I am therefore most decidedly in favor of pushing this policy to the enlistment of a force sufficient to hold all the South falling into our hands and to aid in capturing more."[8]

That other blacks even had the opportunity to volunteer was due in large measure to the men of the Fifty-fourth Massachusetts. Congress awarded fourteen members of the regiment the Medal of Honor, established during the Civil War as the highest military award for bravery, for their courageous assault on Fort Wagner. That battle changed the attitude of many northerners toward the black volunteers and caused them to be more accepting of the notion of black soldiers in the field.

The Fifty-fourth Massachusetts again saw action in February 1864, this time farther south in Florida. The Battle of Olustee also included the Eighty-ninth and Thirty-fifth United States Colored Infantry Regiments. By this time the Bureau of Colored Troops had redesignated all state, Corps d'Afrique, or Louisiana Native Guard units numerically as U.S. Colored Troops. April saw the Battle of Fort Pillow, Tennessee, and the particular danger to which the men of the U.S. Colored Troops subjected themselves by serving their country.

Sergeant William H. Carney of the Massachusetts Fifty-fourth Regiment. When the color sergeant was shot down during the attack on Fort Wagner in South Carolina on July 18, 1863, Carney grasped the flag, led the way to the fort's parapet, and planted the colors there. When the troops fell back, he brought the flag back under fierce fire in which he was twice severely wounded. In 1900, he was awarded the Congressional Medal of Honor for his bravery. (Massachusetts Commandery, Military Order of the Loyal Legion and the U. S. Army Military History Institute)

Helen Amelia Loguen was the daughter of the Reverend Jarmain Loguen, an abolitionist and friend of Frederick Douglass. Helen Amelia and Lewis Douglass, Frederick's son, were sweethearts before the Civil War, and he wrote to her during his time of service with the Fifty-fourth Massachusetts Regiment. After his discharge, he married her. (Onondaga Historical Association)

Letter written by Lewis Douglass to Helen Amelia Loguen when the Fifty-fourth Massachusetts Regiment was stationed at Morris Island, South Carolina, on July 20, 1863.

Fort Pillow was a Union outpost on the Mississippi River defended by some 750 troops, of whom slightly less than half were black. On April 12, 1864, Confederate Major General Nathan Bedford Forrest led an assault on the fort north of Memphis, Tennessee, and demanded its surrender. When the fort's commander refused to surrender, the Confederates stormed the fort, killing, wounding, or capturing nearly all inside it. While about one-third of the white defenders of the fort were killed, some two-thirds of the blacks were butchered, and Union survivors charged that at least some of those murdered blacks had been killed after they had surrendered.

In an April 18, 1864, confrontation at Poison Springs, Arkansas, the Seventy-ninth Colored Infantry suffered nearly twice as many troops killed as wounded, whereas normally in battle, regiments, white or black, suffered more wounded than killed.

The massacres at Fort Pillow and Poison Springs had the effect of spurring the men of the U.S. Colored Troops to even greater valor and determination to win. From then on, their battle cries were "Remember Fort Pillow!" and "Remember Poison Springs!"

These two engagements proved beyond doubt that Confederates were intent on killing the black troops, both in battle and out. Some Confederate regiments deliberately flew a black flag into battle against black Union forces, a sign that they intended to take no black prisoners.

Those black soldiers who were captured by the Confederates

and not murdered were much more severely treated than their fellow white prisoners. One black prisoner of war later recalled that he had so little food that he had to gnaw the leather of old shoes in order to stay alive.

Five

"[Slavery Is] One of Our Chief Sources of Weakness": April 1864–April 1865

As the war's fourth year began, General William Tecumseh Sherman continued his march to Atlanta, Georgia. Sherman, who had succeeded to General Ulysses S. Grant's former position as commander of the western forces when President Lincoln appointed Grant supreme commander of the Union armies, understood that the strategic junction of four important railroads was crucial to supplying the Confederate troops in the western campaign. Between the first of May and the end of August 1864, Sherman's troops destroyed the railroads and cut off the roads leading to Atlanta from both north and south. By late August, they had forced Confederate General John Bell Hood to retreat to Atlanta, and early the following month Sherman's armies overtook that city. The seizure of Atlanta on September 1, 1864, effectively cut the South in half.

In the meantime, Union armies were fighting on a number of fronts, reinforced more and more by black troops. Several famous Union charges involving black troops took place in 1864. More black Union soldiers fought in the Battle of the Crater at Petersburg, Virginia, in late July, than in any other Civil War battle. The Twenty-ninth U.S. Colored Infantry Regiment went into that battle with 450 men and came out with 128. Near Richmond, Virginia, in September, troops from the Fourth and Sixth U.S. Colored Infantry waded through a swamp toward Confederate fortifications with their bayonets fixed, ordered not to fire. But as the Confederates fired on them, the black troops disobeyed orders and

Guard House and Guard, 107th U. S. Colored Infantry, Fort Corcoran, near Washington, D. C. (Library of Congress)

fired back. When they stopped to reload, they were mowed down.

Late in the year, at a railroad bridge over the Big Black River, in Mississippi, Union forces attempted to destroy the bridge so as to cut off the Confederate invasion of Tennessee. Aware of the crucial importance of the bridge, the Confederates had built stockades at each end and had them well-manned with infantry forces. After two attempts by large Union forces failed to gain the bridge, the Third U.S. Colored Infantry was sent in. Major J. B. Cook, commander of the Third, sent two companies to serve as raiding parties. As they waded waist-deep in swamp on each side of the track, they fired a few rounds, then fell back, succeeding in getting the Confederates to fire at the larger Union forces some distance back. The two companies managed to reach the riverbank and at a prearranged signal opened fire on the Confederate forces outside the nearest stockade. While continued fire kept the Confederates inside the stockade from shooting, other Third U.S. Colored Infantry troops began an assault on the stockade by running along the narrow railroad tracks and engaging in hand-to-hand combat. Meanwhile, other black soldiers poured oil onto the bridge and set it afire. Major J. B. Cook was promoted to lieutenant colonel for this daring and heroic victory.

"A Negro Regiment in Action," as illustrated in Harper's Weekly, March 14, 1863. *Photography was still in its infancy at the time of the Civil War, and the heavy cameras and complicated process precluded photographers from capturing battlefield action scenes. (Library of Congress)*

But he could not have done it without his daring and heroic black troops.

Thirteen black regiments fought at Chaffin's Farm in Virginia, at the end of September, their men earning a total of fourteen of the thirty-seven Congressional Medals of Honor awarded to Union troops in that battle.

By October 1864, there were 140 black regiments comprising more than 100,000 men. Although no soldier, white or black, had it easy in the war, the black troops were subjected to particularly grueling conditions. Many of the hardships the U.S. Colored Troops suffered were at the hands of their own officers, fellow white enlisted men, and the Union military structure. Black regiments routinely were issued weapons and other equipment that was inferior to that issued to white troops. Not just shoddy and hodgepodge weapons, but weak pack animals, inedible food, and shoes that wore out in a day were standard fare for black troops. White officers who commanded the black troops were often ashamed of their positions and hated commanding blacks. Some refused to march at the head of their colored troops, as if establishing a physical distance from them could in some way deny the reality of their assignments. They were reluctant to order their black troops into combat and tended to rely on the black regiments under their command to do the menial work of digging ditches and building fortifications. One reason why the black troops often looked scruffier than the white troops was that they were forced to do this dirty work in their uniforms, which they could not afford to replace because they had to buy new uniforms out of their lower pay (in contrast to the white soldiers, who received higher pay as well as new uniforms when needed).

Black troops were more likely than white troops to be assigned duty in unhealthy locations such as southern swamp areas. Military commanders assumed blacks were immune to all tropical diseases. On the contrary, not only were the blacks not immune to tropical diseases, but their more recent arrival on the battlefield meant they had fewer immunities to such diseases as typhoid and cholera that raged through military camps during the Civil War.

When they did have an opportunity to see combat, the black troops were generally good and courageous fighters, in spite of the fact that they were not as experienced in combat as most of the white troops. Their courage stemmed in part from their sure knowledge that they would not survive Confederate capture, but more from the sense that they were at last being afforded the opportunity to fight for a cause that affected them more personally than the white troops. If they proved themselves in battle, they hoped to reap rewards for themselves and their families.

In fact, many white officers preferred to use black troops in brief assaults because of the fierceness with which they fought. White troops were used for longer, more sustained battles because of their greater experience. The drawback for the black troops was that casualties were almost always higher in assaults than they were in sustained battles.

Early in October 1864, the Fifth and Sixth U.S. Colored Cavalry Regiments took part in the Battle of Saltville in Virginia. Colonel James S. Brisbin of the Fifth Regiment reported on the battle in the vicinity of the saltworks, his report serving to illustrate both the hardships the black troops suffered and the bravery they showed in the war.

> *The point to be attacked was the side of a high mountain, the rebels being posted half way up behind rifle-pits made of logs and stones to the height of three feet. All being in readiness, the brigade moved to the attack. The rebels opened upon them a terrific fire, but the line pressed steadily forward up the steep side of the mountain until they found themselves*

within fifty yards of the enemy. Here Colonel Wade [James Wade, of the Sixth U.S. Colored Cavalry] ordered his force to charge, and the negroes rushed upon the works with a yell, and after a desperate struggle carried the entire line, killing and wounding a large number of the enemy and capturing some prisoners. There were 400 black soldiers engaged in the battle, 100 having been left behind sick and with broken-down horses on the march, and 100 having been left in the valley to hold horses. Out of the 400 engaged, 14 men and 4 officers fell killed or wounded. Of this fight I can only say that the men could not have behaved more bravely. I have seen white troops fight in twenty-seven battles and I never saw any fight better. At dusk the colored troops were withdrawn from the enemy's works which they had held for over two hours with scarcely a round of ammunition in their cartridge boxes. On the return of the forces those who had scoffed at the colored troops on the march were silent. Nearly all the wounded were brought off, though we had not an ambulance in the command. The negro soldiers preferred present suffering to being murdered at the hands of a cruel enemy. I saw one man riding with his arm off, another shot through the lungs, another shot through both hips. Such of the colored soldiers as fell into the hands of the enemy during the battle were brutally murdered. The negroes did not retaliate, but treated the rebel wounded with great kindness, carrying them water in their canteens and doing all they could to alleviate the sufferings of those whom the fortunes of war had placed in their hands.[1]

Meanwhile, as the Union navy strengthened its blockades of the Atlantic and Gulf coast ports, Union General William Tecumseh Sherman began a three-hundred-mile march to the Atlantic Ocean through Georgia to Savannah, destroying crucial Confederate supply lines. Slowly, the Confederacy was being starved. Although black troops held back Confederate General John B. Hood's forces in the Battle of Nashville, thus helping to protect Sherman's troops, and black regiments played roles in every other major Union campaign, Sherman's troops were entirely white. As they marched to the Atlantic coast, they destroyed fields, crops, and homes on their way. They also turned away the slaves who sought protection from them. A number of fugitive slaves were subsequently captured by marauding Confederate troops and reenslaved.

General William Tecumseh Sherman, who in August 1864 captured Atlanta, Georgia, and then undertook his famous three-hundred-mile "March to the Sea" to Charleston, South Carolina, destroying crucial Confederate supply lines and effectively starving the South. (Library of Congress)

Sherman's treatment of the slaves caused a scandal in Washington, and President Lincoln sent Secretary of War Edwin M. Stanton to Savannah, Georgia, to investigate the charges. Stanton and Sherman listened as a group of black ministers pleaded that what the slaves needed was land so they could take care of themselves. Four days later, Sherman issued a Field Order setting aside more than four hundred thousand acres of captured Confederate land to be divided among the freed slaves. This was an extraordinary turn of events, showing a sensitivity to the feelings of blacks that the government had never evinced before.

At almost the same time, another extraordinary thing happened: Confederate General Robert E. Lee asked Confederate President Jefferson Davis to be allowed to recruit slaves into the Confederate army, with the promise of freedom for themselves and their families as payment.

Confederate military officials had considered the idea seriously since early 1864. The huge losses the Confederacy had suffered in the course of the war had begun to tell on General Lee and his troops. On January 2, a group of Confederate officers, headed by Major General Patrick R. Cleburne, offered a report to their commanding general. It stated that slavery, once a chief source of Confederate strength, was now "one of our chief sources of weakness." It proposed "that we immediately commence training a large reserve of the most courageous of our slaves, and further that we guarantee freedom within a reasonable time to every slave in the South who shall remain true to the Confederacy in this war." [2]

President Jefferson Davis refused even to consider the proposal and forbade further discussion of the matter in the Confederate army. But the idea would not die. As time went on, and the human, natural, and manufacturing resources of the Confederate states continued to be depleted, more and more people accepted the notion of arming slaves. Indeed, by the fall of 1864, after Rebel defeats in Georgia, Alabama, and Virginia, arming the slaves seemed the only way to save the Confederacy.

As was stated earlier, it was not at all unusual for slaves to be armed, as Marine Lieutenant Henry L. Graves wrote about his slave, Lawrence, in a letter home in late December 1864: "Of Lawrence and his conduct I cannot speak too highly. He . . . was with me in the trenches and Exposed along with me constantly to a hot, sometimes a terrific fire, from the Enemy's Batteries & Sharp Shooters & his indifference to danger and coolness often put to the blush some of the reserve troops who were around us. I got a Rifle for him & he shot many times at the Yanks, who were at times not over 700 yds from us. I was really quite proud of him."[3]

What General Lee and even Judah P. Benjamin, the Confederate secretary of war, wanted was to make the arming of slaves official policy.

But there was also strong opposition to the idea of blacks fighting on the front lines. After all, preserving slavery was one of the reasons the Confederate states had seceded and gone to war. What was the point of arming slaves, who would surely not serve willingly unless their freedom was the incentive for doing so? And if slaves did make courageous soldiers, then the deeply ingrained southern attitude that they were not capable of anything but hard labor was wrong.

Thus, the Confederacy struggled through 1864 relying solely on white fighting forces and using blacks only for manual labor, at least officially.

By early 1865, both sides realized that the war was nearing its end. The situation for the Confederacy was so critical that General Robert E. Lee had become convinced that if slaves were not armed, the cause was lost. He wrote to a Confederate senator on January 11: "If it ends in subverting slavery, it will be accomplished by ourselves, and we can devise the means of alleviating the evil consequences to both races. I think, therefore, we must decide whether slavery shall be extinguished by our enemies and the slave be used against us, or use them ourselves at the risk of the effects which may be produced upon our social institutions. ...We should employ them without delay."[4]

Just over two months later, Confederate President Jefferson Davis gave in and signed an order authorizing the enlistment of slaves as soldiers. This "Negro Soldier Law" provided that slave soldiers could not be freed "except by consent of the owners and of the States in which they may reside."[5]

Ironically, in the same month, Congress finally passed the Thirteenth Amendment to the United States Constitution, prohibiting slavery and all other forms of involuntary servitude. Now, both sides in the war had dealt severe blows to slavery—the South in adopting a policy that would lead to the end of slavery, and the North in actually ending it.

The "Negro Soldier Law" came too late to be of much benefit to the Confederacy. It took time to recruit and organize military regiments. In fact, only a few regiments of slave soldiers had been organized before General

All SLAVES were made FREEMEN.

BY ABRAHAM LINCOLN,

PRESIDENT OF THE UNITED STATES,

JANUARY 1st, 1863.

Come, then, able-bodied COLORED MEN, to the nearest United States Camp, and fight for the

STARS AND STRIPES.

ORIGINAL VERSION
OF THE
JOHN BROWN SONG

The author of the original John Brown Song is H. H. BROWNELL, of Hartford, a nephew of Bishop BROWNELL.

Words that can be sung to the "Hallelujah Chorus."

Old John Brown lies a-mouldering in the grave,
Old John Brown lies slumbering in his grave—
But John Brown's soul is marching with the brave,
    His soul is marching on.
      Glory, Glory, hallelujah !
      Glory, Glory, hallelujah !
      His soul is marching on.

He has gone to be a soldier in the Army of the Lord,
He is sworn as a private in the ranks of the Lord—
He shall stand at Armageddon with his brave old sword,
    When Heaven is marching on.
      Glory, etc.
      For Heaven is marching on.

He shall file in front where the lines of battle form,
He shall face to the front when the squares of battle form,

Time with the column, and charge in the storm,
    When men are marching on.
      Glory, etc.
      True men are marching on.

Ah, foul tyrants ! do you hear him when he comes ?
Ah, black traitors ! do ye know him as he comes ?
In thunder of the cannon and roll of the drums,
    As we go marching on.
      Glory, etc.
      We all are marching on.

Men may die and moulder in the dust—
Men may die, and arise again from dust,
Shoulder to shoulder, in the ranks of the Just,
    When God is marching on.
      Glory, etc.
      The Lord is marching on.

The "John Brown Song" reprinted on this recruitment poster urging "able-bodied Colored Men" to join the Union forces was written in tribute to the martyred abolitionist. It was sung by the United States Colored Troops who entered Richmond, Virginia, the capital of the Confederacy, after that city fell to Union forces in early April 1865. (Library of Congress)

Grant ordered an all-out assault on Petersburg and Richmond, Virginia.

African-American troops were in the vanguard of General Ulysses S. Grant's troops in the assault on Richmond, the Confederate capital. As the rebel forces lost their will to fight, President Jefferson Davis and the rest of the top Confederate government officials fled Richmond, and on April 3 Union troops occupied the city. Members of the black Fifth Massachusetts Cavalry were the first Union soldiers to march into the capital, followed closely by the Twenty-fifth Army Corps, an all-black corps of thirty-two regiments. The black soldiers marched into Richmond carrying the American flag and singing an anthem to the abolitionist martyr John Brown. On April 9, General Lee, with fewer than thirty thousand troops remaining under his command, formally surrendered to General Grant at Appomattox Courthouse near Richmond.

President Abraham Lincoln lived only six days after Lee's surrender to Grant. On April 14 he was shot by an actor named John Wilkes Booth, a Confederate sympathizer who hated Lincoln for bringing about the end of slavery. The president died the following day.

Six

"It Was Midnight and Noonday Without a Space Between": Reconstruction

Before his death, President Abraham Lincoln had begun to draw up plans to reunite the nation. His aim was to readmit the former Rebel states to the Union as quickly as possible and to be as forgiving as possible, for he did not seek revenge on the former secessionists.

But the assassination of Lincoln meant that his plan for bringing the former Confederate states back into the Union was left to his vice president, Andrew Johnson, to carry out once he succeeded to the presidency. Johnson did not have the same leadership abilities as Lincoln, nor the same skills dealing with Congress. Radical Republicans in Congress did seek revenge on the South, and a total transformation of southern society, calling for confiscating the land of the planters and distributing it among ex-slaves. While these radicals failed to achieve their goals, the period of Reconstruction that followed the end of the war was as disruptive in its own way as the war had been.

Federal troops occupied the former Confederate states, which were devastated psychologically and economically. As a condition for readmittance to the Union, the former Confederate states were required to write new constitutions and to ratify three new amendments to the Constitution.

The Thirteenth Amendment (1865) outlawed slavery in the United States.

The Fourteenth Amendment (1868) granted full citizenship rights to blacks and prohibited states from denying them "equal protection of the laws." The amendment did not require states to grant black men the right to vote but provided that those that did not would have their representation in Congress reduced in direct proportion. This provision of the amendment, in addition to Reconstruction laws denying the vote to anyone who had served the Confederacy in an official capacity, whether in the military or in political office, opened the way for northerners and some southern free blacks and former slaves to win election to state Reconstruction governments.

The Fifteenth Amendment (1870) stated, "The right of citizens of the United States to vote shall not be denied or abridged by the United States or by any State on account of race, color, or previous condition of servitude."

Sixteen African Americans were elected to Congress during Reconstruction. Robert Smalls was among them. After the war, Smalls was a member of the Constitutional Convention of South Carolina, which drew up a new constitution for the state as a requirement for its readmission to the Union. He then served two terms in the lower house of the state legislature and two terms in the state senate. In 1876, 1878, 1880, and 1882 he was elected to the United States Congress, serving longer than any other black congressman of the period.

Smalls had joined the South Carolina National Guard in 1869, four years after the Civil War ended, and it was from that state militia that he received the commission of major general. He was never accorded that recognition by the United States Navy, despite his years of brave and devoted service.

Pinckney Benton Stewart Pinchback served as lieutenant governor, and briefly as acting governor, of Louisiana.

The Reconstruction governments established the first public school systems in the South. They also enforced civil rights laws. But they did not have the power to help the majority of southern blacks. Uneducated and unpropertied, the former slaves were ill-equipped to live as free citizens. While the federal Freedmen's Bureau made some attempt to educate and settle the former slaves, its efforts fell woefully short of what needed to be done. Most former slaves wound up working for their former owners, or for other whites, under a sharecropping system that was little better than slavery.

What a tragedy for the former slaves, especially for those who had taken up arms in the cause of their own liberty. In 1888, black Civil War veteran George Washington Williams published *A History of the Negro Troops in the War of the Rebellion, 1861–1865*. In its Preface, he described the profound meaning of Union service for southern slaves, who had stepped ". . . from the Egyptian darkness of bondage to the

"P. B. S. Pinchback, Louisiana (A black J. G. Blaine)." Pinchback, who had served briefly with the Second Louisiana Native Guards, became the highest black office holder during Reconstruction, serving as lieutenant governor and, briefly, as acting governor of Louisiana. During his tenure in these offices, Pinchback was accused of fraud, and the cartoonist's comparison of him with the white Republican politician James G. Blaine may allude to charges against Blaine in 1876 for influence peddling. Another possible reason for the comparison is that Blaine was leader of the "Half-Breed" Republicans, who were against the corrupt patronage of the "Stalwart" Republicans. Pinchback, the son of a white father and a black mother, was called a "half-breed" by those who stooped to personal attacks on his racial heritage. (Author's collection)

lost all hopes. The whole South—every state in the South—had got into the hands of the very men that held us slaves."[3]

The former Confederate states continued to return blacks to virtual slavery. Laws called "black codes," passed by southern legislatures, codified the customary segregation of blacks and whites in all areas of southern life and allowed few if any rights to the black population. In October 1883, the United States Supreme Court decided in what were ironically called the *Civil Rights Cases* that the owner of a place of public accommodation could not be required to admit black patrons because such a requirement would violate the owner's right to private property under the Fourteenth Amendment's due process clause. The Court further ruled that only state legislatures, not the United States Congress, had jurisdiction over a citizen's rights.

A week later, Frederick Douglass said in a speech at Lincoln Hall in Washington, D. C.: "We have been, as a class, grievously wounded, . . . and this wound is too deep and too painful for ordinary measured speech." He characterized the Supreme Court's decision as "one more shocking development of that moral weakness in high places which has attended the conflict between the spirit of liberty and the spirit of slavery." Still, he refused to denounce the government, saying "government is better than

Frederick Douglass with his grandson, Joseph Douglass. Born in slavery, Douglass escaped to the North and became a famous abolitionist. During the Civil War, he worked tirelessly in support of black enlistment in the Union military. (The Schlessinger Library, Radcliffe College)

anarchy, and patient reform is better than violent revolution."[4]

Twelve years later, in 1896, the United States Supreme Court declared segregation the law of the land when it decided, in the case of *Plessy* v. *Ferguson* that separate public accommodations for blacks were constitutional as long as they were "equal."

Frederick Douglass was spared knowledge of the Supreme Court's *Plessy* v. *Ferguson* decision. He died on February 20, 1895, at the age of seventy-eight. But, sadly, he lived to see the white South reestablish its dominance over its black population.

Seven

"Free Without Any Effort of Their Own": Rewriting History

In the first years after the war, there was much residual respect for the black soldiers who had fought on both sides. On the Confederate side, a number of men who as slaves had accompanied their masters to war, or who as free Negroes had served the Confederacy, applied for and received military pensions from the federal government. In the case of the slaves, who were not officially on any military roster, the government required the testimony of whites who had witnessed their service. Quite a few received commendations and were awarded the pensions they sought.

Those who served on the Union side enjoyed greater respect because they had been official members of the Union forces. Nearly 180,000 blacks, organized in more than 150 regiments of cavalry, infantry, and artillery, as well as some 30,000 black sailors (about one-quarter of the navy), had proudly fought for the Union. Without them, the war might have lasted considerably longer than it did; and there was no question that they had tipped the scales in favor of Union victory. After the war, the United States Congress awarded twenty-four of these men (seventeen in the army, seven in the navy) Medals of Honor.

But the military did not really want to retain its black sailors and soldiers. In the fall of 1865, one by one, the United States Colored Troop units were discharged from service. In theory, it was possible for individual black soldiers to remain in the military, but few did. Christian A. Fleetwood, who had attained the rank of sergeant major during his service, and who had been awarded the Congressional Medal of Honor, explained in a June 8, 1865, letter to a friend:

> . . .*I see no good will that will result to our people by contin-*
> *uing to serve. On the contrary it seems to me that our contin-*
> *uing to act in a subordinate capacity with no hope of advance-*
> *ment or promotion is an absolute injury to our cause. It is a*
> *tacit but telling acknowledgement—on our part that we are*
> *not fit for promotion, and that we are satisfied to remain in a*
> *state of marked and acknowledged subservincy.*
>
> > *A double purpose induced me and most others to*
> *enlist, to assist in abolishing slavery and to save the country*
> *from ruin. Something in the furtherance of both objects we*
> *have certainly done and now it strikes me that more could be*
> *done for our welfare in the pursuits of civil life. I think that a*
> *camp life would be decidedly an injury to our people. No mat-*
> *ter how well and faithfully they may perform the duties they*
> *will shortly be considered as 'lazy niggers or as drones in the*
> *great hive.'* [1]

While northern newspapers reminded their readers about the bravery

"Convalescent Colored Troops at Aiken's Landing, M. Aiken's house at right" shows forty black soldiers. Like many other federal militia units, these Union soldiers marched to war clad in uniforms of gray. Colored troops suffered far higher injury and death rates than white troops. (Library of Congress)

of these men for some years after the war, the vast majority of northern towns that erected monuments to Civil War soldiers on their village greens neglected to include those who were black.

As George Washington Williams wrote, "The deathless deeds of the white soldier's valor are not only embalmed in song and story, but are carved in marble and bronze. But nowhere in all this free land is there a monument to brave Negro soldiers, 36,847 of whom gave up their lives in the struggle for national existence."[2]

The one exception was in Boston, where in 1897 a monument to Colonel Robert Gould Shaw and his men of the Fifty-fourth Massachusetts Regiment was erected on Boston Common, forty-five years after the famous assault on Fort Wagner.

A monument to that regiment was a long time in coming, though. The idea first occurred to ex-slaves who lived in the vicinity of Fort Wagner. The autumn after the battle, they raised fifteen hundred dollars for a shaft of granite to be placed on the common grave where the hundreds of soldiers who had died in that battle had been buried. Veterans of the Fifty-fourth matched that sum of money, but the monument was never erected. It was decided, and with good reason, that a monument to black soldiers in South Carolina would never survive

Detail of the memorial to Robert Gould Shaw and the men of the Massachusetts Fifty-fourth Regiment by Augustus Saint-Gaudens. (Houghton Library, Harvard University)

after Union forces were withdrawn.

Not long after the assassination of President Lincoln, Governor John A. Andrew of Massachusetts appointed a committee to raise money for a monument to commemorate the event "by which the title of colored men as 'citizen soldiers' was fixed beyond recall."[3]

But years passed, and as the old abolitionists died out, the idea was shelved. In 1881, Boston architect Henry Hobson Richardson asked why the work had been delayed and got the project rolling again, recommending a sculptor named Augustus Saint-Gaudens. The New Yorker had created a widely praised monument to Admiral Farragut, the Union navy admiral who had captured New Orleans in 1862. Saint-Gaudens's first sketches were of Shaw alone, the colonel on horseback with no depiction of the Negro troops he had commanded. But Shaw's parents objected. Back in 1863, they had refused to have his body buried separately from the black soldiers who had served under him and said they were honored to have him buried with them. Now, they objected that the monument Saint-Gaudens had designed was wrong to honor only Shaw and that he should be directly associated with his troops. So, Saint-Gaudens went back to his drawing board and produced a sketch of a relief sculpture in which the colonel astride his horse is flanked by his men, marching proudly to battle.

Veterans of the Fifty-fourth Massachusetts were invited to the unveiling ceremony. Saint-Gaudens was deeply moved: "... there stood before the relief 65 of these veterans ... the Negro troops ...came in their time-worn frock coats—coats used only on great occasions. Many of them were bent and crippled, many with white [-haired] heads, some with bouquets...They faced and saluted the relief...They seemed as if returning from the war, the troops of bronze marching in the opposite direction, the direction in which they had left for the front, and the young men in bronze showing these veterans the vigor and hope of youth. It was a consecration."[3]

It was also one of the last times the heroics of black veterans of the Civil War came to national attention for one hundred years. Black contributions to the war in which they had the most at stake were left out of history books for the general public and from school textbooks.

Several important books on black contributions to the Civil War were published over the years. There were also articles in such publications as *The Negro History Bulletin*. The February 1944 issue of the *Bulletin* carried an essay by the historian Carter G. Woodson entitled "My Recollections of Veterans of the Civil War." But the facts these books and articles contained did not reach a wide audience and did not erase from the mind of the general public the notion that the Civil War had been a "white man's war." When James M. McPherson's *The Negro's Civil War* was first published in 1965, as he noted in his preface to the 1991 edition, although the crucial role played by blacks in the war was an historical reality, "that reality was not very well known outside the circle of professional historians. . . in the outpouring of books evoked by the Civil War centennial [1961], the number that focused on blacks could be counted on the fingers of one hand—with a finger or two left over."[5]

It would be another thirty years before the contributions of African Americans to the Civil War would be formally recognized by the nation.

In 1993, the National Park Service and the National Archives undertook a huge project, the Civil War Soldiers and Sailors Names Index, a comprehensive list of the 3.5 million men who served in the war. The first phase of the project, an index of the United States Colored Troops, was completed in the summer of 1996. In August 1996, 178,000 names of black soldiers were presented to the African American Civil War Memorial Freedom Foundation for use on its monument to those soldiers. Also provided was a list of the 7,000 white officers who led the U.S. Colored Troops in the Union cause.

It was the plan for such a memorial that led the directors of the CWSS Names Index project to give first priority to the names of the U.S. Colored Troops. In 1992, project managers approached the CWSS Names Index project managers in the hope of obtaining an automated list of names, and since that list was not available, those names became the first phase of the project. At the same time, Howard University initiated an African American Sailors in the Civil War project to develop a similar list for sailors. That list comprises some 50,000 names.

The memorial, designed by Paul Deverovax and Ed Dunson, consists of a three-foot-high semicircular stone wall with stainless steel plaques with the names of the soldiers attached to both sides. On this base stands a bronze cast work containing high- and low-relief sculptures created by Ed Hamilton depicting soldiers from various armed services on the outer side and a family in the inner circle. Groundbreaking for the memorial took place in September 1994. The African American Civil War Memorial is part of the National Park system, whose National Capital Parks Central division includes the Mall, the Washington Monument, and most downtown monuments. It stands as a testament to the crucial role African Americans played in the war that ended slavery, a role that no one will ever forget.

How could African Americans not have tried to be a major part of the effort that led to freedom for all blacks? While they encountered resistance at nearly every turn, they finally succeeded in getting into the fight. The contribution they made to the war that saved the Union also helped to set America on the path to living up to the creed on which the nation was founded: All men are created equal.

The Union victory over the Confederacy and the end of slavery planted the seeds of change in American life and attitudes that finally came to fruition one hundred years later. Due to the courage of black Americans and their white allies in the civil rights movement of the 1960s, a series of civil rights laws were passed that guaranteed full and equal rights to African Americans. Unlike earlier civil rights laws, the Civil Rights Act of 1964 and the Voting Rights Act of 1965 were backed by the full strength and commitment of the federal government. Perhaps more important, they were supported by the majority of the American people.

Notes

Introduction A "White Man's War"?
1. James M. McPherson, *The Negro's Civil War* (New York: Ballantine Books, 1991), p. xv.

Chapter 1 "But This Question Is Still to Be Settled This Negro Question, I Mean. . ."
1. William S. McFeely, *Frederick Douglass.* (New York: W. W. Norton & Co., 1991), p. 205.
2. Bruce Levine et al., eds. *Who Built America? Working People and the Nation's Economy, Politics, Culture, and Society,* Vol. I. (New York: Pantheon Books, 1989), p. 409.
3. *Douglass's Monthly,* May 1861, p. 450.

Chapter 2 "Fighting the Rebels with One Hand": April 1861–April 1862
1. Robert Ewell Greene, *Black Defenders of America,* 1775–1973. (Chicago: Johnson Publishing Co., Inc., 1974), p. 350.
2. *Pittsburgh Gazette,* April 18, 1861; McPherson, pp. 19–20.
3. *The War of the Rebellion: A Compilation of the Official Records of the Union and Confederate Armies,* Series 3, Volume 1, p. 106 (Washington, D.C.: U. S. Government Printing Office, 1892); McPherson, p. 19.

4. Peter H. Clark, *The Black Brigade of Cincinnati.* Cincinnati, 1864, pp. 4–5; McPherson, p. 22.

5. *Douglass's Monthly*, June 1861, p. 469; McPherson, p. 23.

6. *Who Built America?*, p. 429

7. McFeely, pp. 212–213.

8. McPherson, p. 41; *Douglass's Monthly*, IV, August 1861, p. 498.

9. Dorothy Sterling, ed. *Speak Out in Thunder Tones: Letters and Other Writings by Black Northerners, 1787–1865.* (New York: Doubleday & Co., 1973), p. 357.

10. McFeely, p. 213.

Chapter 3 "Men of Color, to Arms!": April 1862–April 1863

1. McPherson, p. 159.

2. Ibid., p. 169.

3. Ibid., p. 62.

4. McFeely, p. 215.

5. Ibid., p. 217.

6. Ibid., p. 218.

7. Clinton Cox, *Undying Glory: The Story of the Massachusetts 54th Regiment* (New York: Scholastic, 1991), pp. 14–15.

8. Ibid., pp. 16–17.

9. McPherson, p. 176.

Chapter 4 "By Arming the Negro We Have Added a Powerful Ally": April 1863-1864

1. *Who Built America?*, p. 435.

2. Joseph T. Glatthaar. *Forged in Battle: The Civil War Alliance of Black Soldiers and White Officers.* (New York: The Free Press, 1990), p. 125.

3. Greene, p. 352.

4. McPherson, p. 189.

5. James Haskins, *America's First Black Governor: P. B. S. Pinchback* (Trenton, NJ: Africa World Press, 1996), p. 25.

6. Peter Burchard, *"We'll Stand by the Union": Robert Gould Shaw and the Black 54th Massachusetts Regiment.* New York: Facts on File, Inc., 1993, p. 92.

7. Ina Chang, *A Separate Battle: Women and the Civil War.* (New York: Lodestar Books, 1991), p. 65.
8. McPherson, p. 195.

Chapter 5 "[Slavery Is] One of Our Chief Sources of Weakness": April **1864**-April **1865**
1. *The War of the Rebellion: A Compilation of the Official Records of the Union and Confederate Armies,*
    Series I, Volume XXXIX. (Washington, D.C.: U.S. Government Printing Office, 1892).
2. McPherson, pp. 245–246.
3. Clarence L. Mohr, *On the Threshold of Freedom: Masters and Slaves in Civil War Georgia.* (Athens:
    University. of Georgia Press, 1986), p. 287.
4. McPherson, p. 248.
5. Op. Cit.

Chapter 6 "It Was Midnight and Noonday Without a Space Between": Reconstruction
1. George Washington Williams, *A History of the Negro Troops in the War of the Rebellion, 1861–1865.*
    (New York: 1888), p. iii.
2. *Who Built America?,* p. 513.
3. Dorothy Sterling, ed. *The Trouble They Seen: Black People Tell the Story of Reconstruction.* (Garden
    City, NY: Doubleday & Co., Inc., 1976), p. 479.
4. McFeely, p. 318.

Chapter 7 "Free Without Any Effort of Their Own": Rewriting History
1. Greene, p. 351.
2. Williams, p. 111.
3. Sidney Kaplan, "The Black Soldier in Literature and Art," *American Studies in Black and White:
    Selected Essays 1949–1989* (Amherst: University of Massachusetts Press, 1991), p. 118.
4. Ibid., p. xi.

Important Dates for the Black, Blue & Gray

1857	The United States Supreme Court rules that Dred Scott, a slave, was not a citizen and could not sue for his freedom in court
1860	
November	Abraham Lincoln elected president of the United States
December	Call issued in Georgia for a convention to deliberate on a confederacy of southern states South Carolina secedes from the Union
1861	
January	Mississippi, Florida, Alabama, Georgia, and Louisiana secede from the Union Kansas admitted to the Union
February	Texas secedes from the Union At a convention in Montgomery, AL, seceded states adopt a Confederate Constitution, elect Jefferson Davis president of the Confederate States

Jefferson Davis is inaugurated on February 18, declaring the new government to be "founded on the opposite idea of the equality of the races"

March   Abraham Lincoln inaugurated as sixteenth president of the United States

April   Confederates fire on Fort Sumter, South Carolina
President Lincoln calls for loyal states to supply troops
Virginia secedes from the Union
Frederick Douglass calls for the recruitment of black troops

May   Arkansas and North Carolina secede from the Union
Union General Benjamin Butler coins the term "contraband" and refuses to surrender slaves who have sought refuge at his command at Fort Monroe, VA

July   First Battle of Bull Run, Manassas, VA

August   President Lincoln declares the Confederate states to be in a state of insurrection
Congress passes the first Confiscation Act, giving the federal government authority to seize property used to aid the rebellion and to free slaves working for the Confederacy

1862
February   Confederate forces evacuate Nashville, TN, making it the first Confederate capital to fall to the Union

April   Battle of Shiloh, Pittsburg Landing, TN
Union Navy Admiral David G. Farragut captures New Orleans

May   General David Hunter, commander of the Department of the South (Georgia, Florida, and South Carolina), issues an Emancipation Proclamation freeing all slaves in those states and also authorizes the arming of ex-slaves. He then organizes the First South Carolina Colored Regiment. Ten days later, President Lincoln disavows General Hunter's emancipation act and the First South Carolina Colored Regiment is disbanded

	Robert Smalls delivers the Confederate supply boat *Planter* to the Union navy
July	The Second Confiscation Act and Militia Act authorize emancipation and employment of fugitive slaves as weapons of war
August	The Second Battle of Bull Run, Manassas, VA
September	Battle of Antietam, Sharpsburg, PA
	President Lincoln issues preliminary Emancipation Proclamation
September– November	First, Second, and Third Louisiana Native Guard Regiments organized and mustered into the Union Army of New Orleans
October	Confederate President Jefferson Davis requests the state of Virginia to draft 4,500 blacks to build fortifications around Richmond
	The First Kansas Colored Volunteer Regiment engages the Confederates at Island Mounds, MO

1863

January	President Abraham Lincoln issues the Emancipation Proclamation, freeing only those slaves in states that had seceded from the Union. Slaves in Union states remain unaffected
	Governor John A. Andrew of Massachusetts authorized by Secretary of War Edwin M. Stanton to recruit and organize black soldiers
	The First South Carolina Volunteer Regiment engages the enemy at Township FI
March	Frederick Douglass issues a declaration: "Men of Color, to Arms!", and begins to recruit troops
	Secretary of War Stanton authorizes the organization of black troops into the Mississippi Valley
	Fifty-Fourth Regiment Massachusetts Volunteers mustered into the Union army
May	Union General William Tecumseh Sherman begins his march toward Atlanta, GA
	First Kansas Colored Volunteer Regiment engages the enemy at Sherwood, MO

	Confederate victory at Chancellorsville, VA
	The War Department establishes a Bureau of Colored Troops
May–July	Battle of Port Hudson, LA; the Union forces in that battle include two Louisiana Native Guards and six corps d'Afrique regiments
June	Battle of Milliken's Bend, LA. Union forces include the Ninth and Eleventh Louisiana Colored Volunteer and First Mississippi Colored Volunteer Regiments
July	Battle of Gettysburg, PA
	Vicksburg, MS, falls to Union forces
	Draft riots in New York City
	Battle of Honey Springs (Elk Creek) in Indian Territory; Union forces include First Kansas Colored Volunteer Regiment
	Assault on Fort Wagner, South Carolina, by Fifty-fourth Massachusetts Volunteer Regiment

1864

February	Battle of Olustee, Florida; Union forces include the Fifty-fourth Massachusetts Volunteer and the Eighty-ninth and Thirty-fifth United States Colored Infantry Regiments
April	Thirteenth Amendment to the United States Constitution, outlawing slavery, passes the U. S. Senate
	Massacre of Union soldiers—black enlisted and white officers—at Fort Pillow, TN
June–July	U. S. House of Representatives fails to pass Thirteenth Amendment; President Lincoln announces his support of it
	War Department equalizes wages for black and white troops
September	Atlanta, GA, falls to the Union
	Confederate General Robert E. Lee, in a letter to President Jefferson Davis, advises the use of blacks in support services in the Confederate army
	Battle of Chaffin's Farm, New Market Heights, VA; twelve U. S. Colored Infantry

regiments and one Cavalry regiment are involved in the battle, and thirteen men in the U.S. Colored Infantry regiments are awarded the Congressional Medal of Honor

November	President Lincoln reelected
	Battle of Honey Hills, SC. Union forces include the Fifty-fourth and Fifty-fifth Massachusetts Volunteer and Thirty-second, Thirty-fifth, and One-hundred and second U.S. Colored Infantry Regiments
December	The Twenty-fifth Army Corps organized; first and only army corps made up of all black infantry regiments

1865

April	Richmond, VA, falls to the Union
	Confederate General Robert E. Lee surrenders to Union General Ulysses S. Grant at Appomattox, VA
	President Lincoln is shot by John Wilkes Booth and dies the following day
December	Thirteenth Amendment ratified after approval by twenty-seven states
1866	Congress passes a civil rights bill designed to protect Negroes from Black Codes and other discriminatory efforts in the South
	Congress passes the Fourteenth Amendment, according blacks full citizenship and equal protection under the law
1867	Congress enacts the first Reconstruction Act
1868	Fourteenth Amendment to the Constitution ratified; declares all persons born or naturalized in the United States to be citizens
1870	Fifteenth Amendment to the Constitution ratified; guarantees black men the right to vote

1875   Congress passes the Civil Rights Act

1877   Reconstruction officially ends when newly elected President Rutherford B. Hayes orders the withdrawal of all federal troops from the former Confederate states

1895   In *Plessy v. Ferguson*, United States Supreme Court rules that separate accommodations may be provided for blacks, as long as they are "equal"

African-American Medal of Honor Recipients in the Civil War

(Source: Medal of Honor Historical Society, Mesa, Arizona)

Army

Anderson, Bruce (?–August 24, 1922). Date earned January 15, 1865; awarded December 28, 1914

Barnes, William (?–December 24, 1866 while on active duty). Date earned September 29, 1864; awarded April 6, 1865

Beaty, Powhatan (October 8, 1838–September 29, 1864). Date earned September 29, 1864; awarded April 6, 1865

Bronson, James H. (?–March 16, 1884). Date earned September 29, 1864; awarded April 6, 1865

Carney, William H. (February 29, 1840–December 9, 1908). Date earned July 18, 1863; awarded May 23, 1900

Dorsey, Decatur (1836–July 11, 1891). Date earned July 30, 1864; awarded November 8, 1865

Fleetwood, Christian A. (July 21, 1840–September 28, 1914). Date earned September 29, 1864; awarded April 6, 1865

Gardiner, James (September 16, 1839–September 29, 1905). Date earned September 29, 1864; awarded April 6, 1865

Harris, James H. (?–January 28, 1898). Date earned September 29, 1864; awarded February 18, 1874

Hawkins, Thomas R. (?–February 28, 1870). Date earned September 29, 1864; awarded February 8, 1870

Hilton, Alfred B. (?–Killed in action October 21, 1864). Date earned September 29, 1864; awarded April 6, 1865

Holland, Milton M. (1844–May 15, 1910). Date earned September 29, 1864; awarded April 6, 1865

James, Miles (?–August 28, 1871). Date earned September 30, 1864; awarded April 6, 1865

Kelly, Alexander (July 7, 1840–June 19, 1907). Date earned September 29, 1864; awarded April 6, 1865

Pinn, Robert A. (March 1, 1843–January 1, 1911). Date earned September 29, 1864; awarded April 6, 1865

Ratcliff, Edward (?–March 10, 1915). Date earned September 29, 1864; awarded April 6, 1865

Veal, Charles (?–July 27, 1872). Date earned September 29, 1864; awarded April 6, 1865

Navy

Blake Robert (?–?). Date earned December 25, 1863; award date not available

Brown, William H. (1836–November 5, 1896). Date earned August 5, 1864; award date not available

Brown, Wilson (1841–January 24, 1900). Date earned August 5, 1864; award date not available

Lawson, John (June 16, 1837–May 3, 1919) Date earned August 5, 1864; awarded April 23, 1865

Mifflin, James (1839–?). Date earned August 5, 1864; award date not available.

Pease, Joachim (?–?). Date earned June 19, 1864; award date not available

Sanderson, Aaron (indicated in some sources as Anderson, Aaron), (?–?). Date earned March 17, 1865; awarded February 6, 1867

Bibliography

Berlin, Ira, ed. *Free at Last: A Documentary History of Slavery, Freedom, and the Civil War.* New York: The New Press, 1992.

Boles, John B. *Black Southerners 1619–1869.* Lexington, KY: The University Press of Kentucky, 1983.

Burchard, Peter. *"We'll Stand by the Union": Robert Gould Shaw and the Black 54th Massachusetts Regiment.* New York: Facts On File, Inc., 1993.

Chang, Ina. *A Separate Battle: Women and the Civil War.* New York: Lodestar Books, 1991.

Cornish, Dudley Taylor. *The Sable Arm: Negro Troops in the Union Army, 1861–1865.* New York: W. W. Norton & Co., Inc., 1966.

Cox, Clinton. *Undying Glory: The Story of the Massachusetts 54th Regiment.* New York: Scholastic, 1991.

Glatthaar, Joseph T. *Forged in Battle: The Civil War Alliance of Black Soldiers and White Officers.* New York: The Free Press, 1990.

Greene, Robert Ewell. *Black Defenders of America, 1775–1973.* Chicago: Johnson Publishing Co., Inc., 1974.

Haskins, James. *America's First Black Governor: P. B. S. Pinchback.* Trenton, NJ: Africa World Press, Inc., 1996.

Haskins, Jim. *Get On Board: The Story of the Underground Railroad.* New York: Scholastic, 1992.

Higginson, Thomas Wentworth. *Army Life in a Black Regiment.* Williamstown, MA: Corner House Publishers, 1971.

Kaplan, Sidney. "The Black Soldier in Literature and Art," *American Studies in Black and White: Selected Essays 1949–1989.* Amherst: University of Massachusetts Press, 1991.

_____. *The Black Presence in the Era of the Revolution, 1770–1800*. New York: The New York Graphic Society, Ltd., 1973.

Levine, Bruce, et al., eds. *Who Built America? Working People and the Nation's Economy, Politics, Culture, and Society*, Vol. I. New York: Pantheon Books, 1989.

McFeely, William S. *Frederick Douglass*. New York: W. W. Norton & Co., Inc., 1991.

McPherson, James M. *Battle Cry of Freedom: The Civil War Era*. New York: Oxford University Press, 1988.

_____. *The Negro's Civil War*. New York: Ballantine Books, 1991.

Mohr, Clarence L. *On the Threshold of Freedom: Masters and Slaves in Civil War Georgia*. Athens, GA: University of Georgia Press, 1986.

Murphy, Jim. *The Boys' War: Confederate and Union Soldiers Talk About the Civil War*. New York: Scholastic, 1991.

Sterling, Dorothy, ed. *Speak Out in Thunder Tones: Letters and Other Writings by Black Northerners, 1787–1865*. New York: Doubleday & Co., Inc., 1973.

Williams, George W. *A History of the Negro Troops in the War of the Rebellion, 1861–1865*. New York: Kraus Reprint Company, 1969.

_____. *The History of the Negro Race in America 1619–1880*. New York: Arno Press & The New York Times, 1968.

Woodson, Carter G. "My Recollections of Veterans of the Civil War", *The Negro History Bulletin*, February 1944.

Index

Photo Acknowledgments

Page 9: Library of Congress
Page 11: Schomburg Center for Research in Black Culture, New York Public Library
Page 16: Library of Congress
Page 26: Library of Congress
Page 33: Library of Congress
Page 40: Library of Congress
Page 45: Library of Congress
Page 47: Library of Congress
Page 49: Library of Congress
Page 52: Library of Congress
Page 55: Library of Congress
Page 61: Library of Congress
Page 66: Library of Congress
Page 74: Metropolitan Museum of Art, Gift of Charles Stewart Smith, 1884 (84.12c)
Page 75: Metropolitan Museum of Art, Gift of Charles Stewart Smith, 1884 (84.12c)
Page 75: Metropolitan Museum of Art, Gift of Charles Stewart Smith, 1884 (84.12c)
Page 77: Library of Congress
Page 90: Massachusetts Commandery, Military Order of the Loyal Legion and the US Army Military History Institute
Page 93: Massachusetts Commandery, Military Order of the Loyal Legion and the US   Army Military History Institute
Page 94: Onondaga Historical Association
Page 95: Library of Congress
Page 100: Library of Congress
Page 102: Library of Congress
Page 108: Library of Congress
Page 113: Library of Congress
Page 119: Collection of Jim Haskins
Page 123: The Schlessinger Library, Radcliffe College
Page 128: Library of Congress
Page 130: By permission of the Houghton Library, Harvard University